ANNA KATHARINE (ROHLFS) GREEN

A Difficult Problem; The Staircase at the Heart's Delight and Other Stories

The American Short Story Series

VOLUME 16

GARRETT PRESS

Library of Congress Catalog Card No. 68-55686

This volume was reprinted from the 1900 edition published by The F.M. Lupton Publishing Co.

First Garrett Press Edition published 1969

The American Short Story Series
Volume 16

Manufactured in the United States of America

250 West 54th Street, New York, N.Y. 10019

CONTENTS

PAGE

A DIFFICULT PROBLEM 7
THE GRAY MADAM 55
THE BRONZE HAND 97
- I. The Fascinating Unknown 99
- II. The Quaker-like Girl, the Pale Girl, and the Man with a Bristling Moustache 116
- III. Madame 132
- IV. Checkmate 152
- V. Doctor Merriam 165
- VI. The Box Again 171

MIDNIGHT IN BEAUCHAMP ROW 191
THE STAIRCASE AT THE HEART'S DELIGHT 221
THE HERMIT OF —— STREET 261
- I. I Commit an Indiscretion 263
- II. A Strange Wedding Breakfast 283
- III. One Bead from a Necklace 303
- IV. I Learn Hypocrisy 310
- V. The Stolen Key 313
- VI. While Others Danced 331

A DIFFICULT PROBLEM

I.

"A LADY to see you, sir."

I looked up and was at once impressed by the grace and beauty of the person thus introduced to me.

"Is there anything I can do to serve you?" I asked, rising.

She cast me a child-like look full of trust and candor as she seated herself in the chair I pointed out to her.

"I believe so, I hope so," she earnestly assured me. "I—I am in great trouble. I have just lost my husband—but it is not that. It is the slip of paper I found on my dresser, and which—which——"

She was trembling violently and her words were fast becoming incoherent. I calmed her and asked her to relate her story just as it had happened; and after a few minutes of silent struggle she succeeded in collecting herself sufficiently to respond with some degree of connection and self-possession.

"I have been married six months. My name is Lucy Holmes. For the last few weeks my husband and myself have been living in an apartment house on Fifty-ninth Street, and as we had not a care in the world, we were very happy till Mr. Holmes was called away on business to Philadelphia. This was two weeks ago. Five days later I received an affectionate letter from him, in which he promised to come back the next day; and the news so delighted me that I accepted an invitation to the theater from some intimate friends of ours. The next morning I naturally felt fatigued and rose late; but I was very cheerful, for I expected my husband at noon. And now comes the perplexing mystery. In the course of dressing myself I stepped to my bureau, and seeing a small newspaper-slip attached to the cushion by a pin, I drew it off and read it. It was a death notice, and my hair rose and my limbs failed me as I took in its fatal and incredible words.

"'Died this day at the Colonnade, James Forsythe De Witt Holmes. New York papers please copy.'

"James Forsythe De Witt Holmes was my husband, and his last letter, which was at that very moment lying beside the cushion, had been dated from the Colonnade. Was I dreaming or under the spell of some frightful hallucination which led me to misread the name on the slip of paper before me? I could not determine. My head, throat and chest seemed bound about with iron, so that I could neither speak nor breathe with freedom, and, suffering thus, I stood staring at this demoniacal bit of paper which in an instant had brought the shadow of death upon my happy life. Nor was I at all relieved when a little later I flew with the notice into a neighbor's apartment, and praying her to read it for me, found that my eyes had not deceived me and that the name was indeed my husband's and the notice one of death.

"Not from my own mind but from hers came the first suggestion of comfort.

"'It cannot be your husband who is meant,' said she; 'but some one of the same name. Your husband wrote to you yesterday, and this person must have been dead at least two days for the printed notice of his decease to have reached New York. Some one has remarked the striking similarity of names, and wishing to startle you, cut the slip out and pinned it on your cushion.'

"I certainly knew of no one inconsiderate enough to do this, but the explanation was so plausible, I at once embraced it and sobbed aloud in my relief. But in the midst of my rejoicing I heard the bell ring in my apartment, and running thither, encountered a telegraph boy holding in his outstretched hand the yellow envelope which so often bespeaks death or disaster. The sight took my breath away. Summoning my maid, whom I saw hastening towards me from an inner room, I begged her to open the telegram for me. Sir, I saw in her face, before she had read the first line, a confirmation of my very worst fears. My husband was——"

The young widow, choked with her emotions, paused, recovered herself for the second time, and then went on.

"I had better show you the telegram."

Taking it from her pocket-book, she held it towards me. I read it at a glance. It was short, simple and direct.

"Come at once. Your husband found dead in his room this morning. Doctors say heart disease. Please telegraph."

"You see it says this morning," she explained, placing her delicate finger on the word she so eagerly quoted. "That means a week ago Wednesday, the same day on which the printed slip recording his death was found on my cushion. Do you not see something very strange in this?"

I did; but, before I ventured to express myself on this subject, I desired her to tell me what she had learned in her visit to Philadelphia.

Her answer was simple and straightforward.

"But little more than you find in this telegram. He died in his room. He was found lying on the floor near the bell button, which he had evidently risen to touch. One hand was clenched on his chest, but his face wore a peaceful look as if death had come too suddenly to cause him much suffering. His bed was undisturbed; he had died before retiring, possibly in the act of packing his trunk, for it was found nearly ready for the expressman. Indeed, there was every evidence of his intention to leave on an early morning train. He had even desired to be awakened at six o'clock; and it was his failure to respond to the summons of the bell-boy, which led to so early a discovery of his death. He had never complained of any distress in breathing, and we had always considered him a perfectly healthy man; but there was no reason for assigning any other cause than heart-failure to his sudden death, and so the burial certificate was made out to that effect, and I was allowed to bring him home and bury him in our vault at Woodlawn. But—" and here her earnestness dried up the tears which had been flowing freely during this recital of her husband's lonely death and sad burial,—"do you not think an investigation should be made into a death preceded by a false obituary notice? For I found when I was in Philadelphia that no paragraph such as I had found pinned to my cushion had been inserted in any paper there, nor had any other man of the same name ever registered at the Colonnade, much less died there."

"Have you this notice with you?" I asked.

She immediately produced it, and while I was glancing it over remarked:

"Some persons would give a superstitious explanation to the whole matter; think I had received a supernatural warning and been satisfied with what they would call a spiritual manifestation. But I have not a bit of such folly in my composition. Living hands set up the type and printed the words which gave me so deathly a shock; and hands, with a real purpose in them, cut it from the paper and pinned it to my cushion for me to see when I woke on that fatal morning. But whose hands? That is what I want you to discover."

I had caught the fever of her suspicions long before this and now felt justified in showing my interest.

"First, let me ask," said I, "who has access to your rooms besides your maid?"

"No one; absolutely no one."

"And what of her?"

"She is innocence itself. She is no common housemaid, but a girl my mother brought up, who for love of me consents to do such work in the household as my simple needs require."

"I should like to see her."

"There is no objection to your doing so;

but you will gain nothing by it. I have already talked the subject over with her a dozen times and she is as much puzzled by it as I am myself. She says she cannot see how any one could have found an entrance to my room during my sleep, as the doors were all locked. Yet, as she very naturally observes, some one must have done so, for she was in my bedroom herself just before I returned from the theater, and can swear, if necessary, that no such slip of paper was to be seen on my cushion, at that time, for her duties led her directly to my bureau and kept her there for full five minutes."

"And you believed her?" I suggested.

"Implicitly."

"In what direction, then, do your suspicions turn?"

"Alas! in no direction. That is the trouble. I don't know whom to mistrust. It was because I was told that you had the credit of seeing light where others can see nothing but darkness, that I have sought your aid in this emergency. For the uncertainty surrounding this matter is killing me and will make my sorrow quite unendurable if I cannot obtain relief from it."

"I do not wonder," I began, struck by the note of truth in her tones. "And I shall certainly do what I can for you. But before we go any further, let us examine this scrap of newspaper and see what we can make out of it."

I had already noted two or three points in connection with it, to which I now proceeded to direct her attention.

"Have you compared this notice," I pursued, "with such others as you find every day in the papers?"

"No," was her eager answer. "Is it not like them all——"

"Read," was my quiet interruption. "'On this day at the Colonnade—' On what day? The date is usually given in all the *bona-fide* notices I have seen."

"Is it?" she asked, her eyes moist with unshed tears, opening widely in her astonishment.

"Look in the papers on your return home and see. Then the print. Observe that the type is identical on both sides of this make-believe clipping, while in fact there is always a perceptible difference between that used in the obituary column and that to be found in the columns devoted to other matter. Notice also," I continued, holding up the scrap of paper between her and the light, "that the alignment on one side is not exactly parallel with that on the other; a discrepancy which would not exist if both sides had been printed on a newspaper press. These facts lead me to conclude, first, that the effort to match the type exactly was the mistake of a man who tries to do too much; and secondly, that one of the sides at least, presumably that containing the obituary notice, was printed on a hand-press, on the blank side of a piece of galley proof picked up in some newspaper office."

"Let me see." And stretching out her hand with the utmost eagerness, she took the slip and turned it over. Instantly a change took place in her countenance. She sank back in her seat and a blush of manifest confusion suffused her cheeks. "Oh!" she exclaimed, "what will you think of me! I brought this scrap of print into the house *myself*, and it was *I* who pinned it on the cushion with my own hands! I remember it now. The sight of those words recalls the whole occurrence."

"Then there is one mystery less for us to solve," I remarked, somewhat dryly.

"Do you think so," she protested, with a deprecatory look. "For me the mystery deepens, and becomes every minute more serious. It is true that I brought this scrap of newspaper into the house, and that it had, then as now, the notice of my husband's death upon it, but the time of my bringing it in was Tuesday night, and he was not found dead till Wednesday morning."

"A discrepancy worth noting," I remarked.

"Involving a mystery of some importance," she concluded.

I agreed to that.

"And since we have discovered how the slip came into your room, we can now proceed to the clearing up of this mystery," I observed. "You can, of course, inform me where you procured this clipping which you say you brought into the house?"

"Yes. You may think it strange, but when I alighted from the carriage that night, a man on the sidewalk put this tiny scrap of paper into my hand. It was done so mechanically that it made no more impression on my mind than the thrusting of an advertisement upon me. Indeed, I supposed it was an advertisement, and I only wonder that I retained it in my hand at all. But that I did do so, and that, in a moment of abstraction I went so far as to pin it to my cushion, is evident from the fact that a vague memory remains in my mind of having read this recipe which you see printed on the reverse side of the paper."

"It was the recipe, then, and not the obituary notice which attracted your attention the night before?"

"Probably, but in pinning it to the cushion, it was the obituary notice that chanced to come uppermost. Oh, why should I not have remembered this till now! Can you understand my forgetting a matter of so much importance?"

"Yes," I allowed, after a momentary consideration of her ingenuous countenance. "The words you read in the morning were so startling that they disconnected themselves from those you had carelessly glanced at the night before."

"That is it," she replied; "and since then I have had eyes for the one side only. How could I think of the other? But who could have printed this thing and who was the man who put it into my hand? He looked like a beggar but— Oh!" she suddenly exclaimed, her cheeks flushing scarlet and her eyes flashing with a feverish, almost alarming, glitter.

"What is it now?" I asked. "Another recollection?"

"Yes." She spoke so low I could hardly hear her. "He coughed and——"

"And what?" I encouragingly suggested, seeing that she was under some new and overwhelming emotion.

"That cough had a familiar sound, now that I think of it. It was like that of a friend who-- But no, no; I will not wrong him by any false surmises. He would stoop to much, but not to that; yet——"

The flush on her cheeks had died away, but the two vivid spots which remained showed the depth of her excitement.

"Do you think," she suddenly asked, "that a man out of revenge might plan to frighten me by a false notice of my husband's death, and that God to punish him, made the notice a prophecy?"

"I think a man influenced by the spirit of revenge might do almost anything," I answered, purposely ignoring the latter part of her question.

"But I always considered him a good man.

At least I never looked upon him as a wicked one. Every other beggar we meet has a cough; and yet," she added after a moment's pause, "if it was not he who gave me this mortal shock, who was it? He is the only person in the world I ever wronged."

"Had you not better tell me his name?" I suggested.

"No, I am in too great doubt. I should hate to do him a second injury."

"You cannot injure him if he is innocent. My methods are very safe."

"If I could forget his cough! but it had that peculiar catch in it that I remembered so well in the cough of John Graham. I did not pay any especial heed to it at the time. Old days and old troubles were far enough from my thoughts; but now that my suspicions are raised, that low, choking sound comes back to me in a strangely persistent way, and I seem to see a well-remembered form in the stooping figure of this beggar. Oh, I hope the good God will forgive me if I attribute to this disappointed man a wickedness he never committed."

"Who is John Graham?" I urged, "and what was the nature of the wrong you did him?"

She rose, cast me one appealing glance, and perceiving that I meant to have her whole story, turned towards the fire and stood warming her feet before the hearth, with her face turned away from my gaze.

"I was once engaged to marry him," she began. "Not because I loved him, but because we were very poor—I mean my mother and myself—and he had a home and seemed both good and generous. The day came when we were to be married—this was in the West, way out in Kansas—and I was even dressed for the wedding, when a letter came from my uncle here, a rich uncle, very rich, who had never had anything to do with my mother since her marriage, and in it he promised me fortune and everything else desirable in life if I would come to him, unencumbered by any foolish ties,

Think of it! And I within half an hour of marriage with a man I had never loved and now suddenly hated. The temptation was overwhelming, and heartless as my conduct may appear to you, I succumbed to it. Telling my lover that I had changed my mind, I dismissed the minister when he came, and announced my intention of proceeding East as soon as possible. Mr. Graham was simply paralyzed by his disappointment, and during the few days which intervened before my departure, I was haunted by his face, which was like that of a man who had died from some overwhelming shock. But when I was once free of the town, especially after I arrived in New York, I forgot alike his misery and himself. Everything I saw was so beautiful! Life was so full of charm, and my uncle so delighted with me and everything I did! Then there was James Holmes, and after I had seen him— But I cannot talk of that. We loved each other, and under the surprise of this new delight how could I be expected to remember the man

I had left behind me in that barren region in which I had spent my youth? But he did not forget the misery I had caused him. He followed me to New York: and on the morning I was married found his way into the house, and mixing with the wedding guests, suddenly appeared before me just as I was receiving the congratulations of my friends. At sight of him I experienced all the terror he had calculated upon causing, but remembering at whose side I stood, I managed to hide my confusion under an aspect of apparent haughtiness. This irritated John Graham. Flushing with anger, and ignoring my imploring look, he cried peremptorily, 'Present me to your husband!' and I felt forced to present him. But his name produced no effect upon Mr. Holmes. I had never told him of my early experience with this man, and John Graham, perceiving this, cast me a bitter glance of disdain and passed on, muttering between his teeth, 'False to me and false to him! Your punishment be upon you!' and I felt as if I had been cursed."

She stopped here, moved by emotions readily to be understood. Then with quick impetuosity she caught up the thread of her story and went on.

"That was six months ago; and again I forgot. My mother died and my husband soon absorbed my every thought. How could I dream that this man, who was little more than a memory to me and scarcely that, was secretly planning mischief against me? Yet this scrap about which we have talked so much may have been the work of his hands; and even my husband's death——"

She did not finish, but her face, which was turned towards me, spoke volumes.

"Your husband's death shall be inquired into," I assured her. And she, exhausted by the excitement of her discoveries, asked that she might be excused from further discussion of the subject at that time.

As I had no wish, myself, to enter any more fully into the matter just then, I readily acceded to her request, and the pretty widow left me.

II.

OBVIOUSLY the first fact to be settled was whether Mr. Holmes had died from purely natural causes. I accordingly busied myself the next few days with this question, and was fortunate enough to so interest the proper authorities that an order was issued for the exhumation and examination of the body.

The result was disappointing. No traces of poison were to be found in the stomach nor was there to be seen on the body any mark of violence, with the exception of a minute prick upon one of his thumbs.

This speck was so small that it escaped every eye but my own.

The authorities assuring the widow that the doctor's certificate given her in Philadelphia was correct, he was again interred. But I was not satisfied; neither do I think she was. I was confident that his death was not a natural one, and entered upon one of those secret and prolonged investigations which have constituted the pleasure of my life for so many years. First, I visited the Colonnade in Philadelphia, and being allowed to see the room in which Mr. Holmes died, went through it carefully. As it had not been used since that time I had some hopes of coming upon a clue.

But it was a vain hope and the only result of my journey to this place was the assurance I received that the gentleman had spent the entire evening preceding his death, in his own room, where he had been brought several letters and one small package, the latter coming by mail. With this one point gained—if it was a point—I went back to New York.

Calling on Mrs. Holmes, I asked her if, while her husband was away she had sent him anything besides letters, and upon her replying to the contrary, requested to know if in her visit to Philadelphia she had noted among her husband's effects anything that was new or unfamiliar to her. "For he received a package while there," I explained, "and though its contents may have been perfectly harmless, it is just as well for us to be assured of this, before going any further."

"Oh, you think, then, he was really the victim of some secret violence."

"We have no proof of it," I said. "On the contrary, we are assured that he died from natural causes. But the incident of the newspaper slip outweighs, in my mind, the doctor's conclusions, and until the mystery surrounding that obituary notice has been satisfactorily explained by its author, I shall hold to the theory that your husband has been made away with in some strange and seemingly unaccountable manner, which it is our duty to bring to light."

"You are right! You are right! Oh, John Graham!"

She was so carried away by this plain expression of my belief that she forgot the question I had put to her.

"You have not told whether or not you

found anything among your husband's effects that can explain this mystery," I suggested.

She at once became attentive.

"Nothing," said she: "his trunks were already packed and his bag nearly so. There were a few things lying about the room which were put into the latter, but I saw nothing but what was familiar to me among them; at least, I think not; perhaps we had better look through his trunk and see. I have not had the heart to open it since I came back."

As this was exactly what I wished, I said as much, and she led me into a small room, against the wall of which stood a trunk with a traveling-bag on top of it. Opening the latter, she spread the contents out on the trunk.

"I know all these things," she sadly murmured, the tears welling in her eyes.

"This?" I inquired, lifting up a bit of coiled wire with two or three little rings dangling from it.

"No; why, what is that?"

"It looks like a puzzle of some kind."

"Then it is of no consequence. My husband was forever amusing himself over some such contrivance. All his friends knew how well he liked these toys and frequently sent them to him. This one evidently reached him in Philadelphia."

Meanwhile I was eying the bit of wire curiously. It was undoubtedly a puzzle, but it had appendages to it that I did not understand.

"It is more than ordinarily complicated," I observed, moving the rings up and down in a vain endeavor to work them off.

"The better he would like it," said she.

I kept on working with the rings. Suddenly I gave a painful start. A little prong in the handle of the toy had started out and pricked me.

"You had better not handle it," said I, and laid it down. But the next minute I took it up again and put it in my pocket. The prick made by this treacherous bit of mechanism was in or near the same place on my thumb as the one I had noticed on the hand of the deceased Mr. Holmes.

There was a fire in the room, and before proceeding further, I cauterized that prick with the end of a red-hot poker. Then I made my adieux to Mrs. Holmes and went immediately to a chemist friend of mine.

"Test the end of this bit of steel for me," said I. "I have reason to believe it carries with it a deadly poison."

He took the toy, promised to subject it to every test possible and let me know the result. Then I went home. I felt ill, or imagined that I did, which under the circumstances was almost as bad.

Next day, however, I was quite well, with the exception of a certain inconvenience in my thumb. But not till the following week did I receive the chemist's report. It overthrew my whole theory. He had found nothing, and returned me the bit of steel.

But I was not convinced.

"I will hunt up this John Graham," thought I, "and study him."

But this was not so easy a task as it may appear. As Mrs. Holmes possessed no clue to the whereabouts of her quondam lover, I had nothing to aid me in my search for him, save her rather vague description of his personal appearance and the fact that he was constantly interrupted in speaking by a low, choking cough. However, my natural perseverance carried me through. After seeing and interviewing a dozen John Grahams without result, I at last lit upon a man of that name who presented a figure of such vivid unrest and showed such desperate hatred of his fellows, that I began to entertain hopes of his being the person I was in search of. But determined to be sure of this before proceeding further, I confided my suspicions to Mrs. Holmes, and induced her to accompany me down to a certain spot on the "Elevated" from which I had more than once seen this man go by to his usual lounging place in Printing-house Square.

She showed great courage in doing this, for she had such a dread of him that she was in a state of nervous excitement from the moment she left her house, feeling sure that she would attract his attention and thus risk a disagreeable encounter. But she might have spared herself these fears. He did not even glance up in passing us, and it was mainly by his walk she recognized him. But she did recognize him ; and this nerved me at once to set about the formidable task of fixing upon him a crime which was not even admitted as a fact by the authorities.

He was a man-about-town, living, to all appearance, by his wits. He was to be seen mostly in the downtown portions of the city, standing for hours in front of some newspaper office, gnawing at his finger-ends, and staring at the passers-by with a hungry look that alarmed the timid and provoked alms from the benevolent. Needless to say that he rejected the latter expression of sympathy, with angry contempt.

His face was long and pallid, his cheek-bones high and his mouth bitter and resolute in expression. He wore neither beard nor mustache, but made up for their lack by an abundance of light brown hair, which hung very nearly to his shoulders. He stooped in standing, but as soon as he moved, showed decision and a certain sort of pride which caused him to hold his head high and his body more than usually erect. With all these good points his appearance was decidedly sinister, and I did not wonder that Mrs. Holmes feared him.

My next move was to accost him. Pausing before the doorway in which he stood, I addressed him some trivial question. He answered me with sufficient politeness, but with a grudging attention which betrayed the hold which his own thoughts had upon him. He coughed while speaking and his eye, which for a moment rested on mine, produced upon me an impression for which I was hardly prepared, great as was my prejudice against him. There was such an icy composure in it; the composure of an envenomed nature conscious of its superiority to all surprise. As I lingered to study him more closely, the many dangerous qualities of the man became more and more apparent to me ; and convinced that to proceed further without deep and careful thought, would be to court failure where triumph would set me up for life, I gave up all present attempt at enlisting him in conversation, and went my way in an inquiring and serious mood.

In fact, my position was a peculiar one, and the problem I had set for myself one of unusual difficulty. Only by means of some extraordinary device such as is seldom resorted to by the police of this or any other nation, could I hope to arrive at the secret of this man's conduct, and triumph in a matter which to all appearance was beyond human penetration.

But what device? I knew of none, nor through two days and nights of strenuous thought did I receive the least light on the subject. Indeed, my mind seemed to grow more and more confused the more I urged it into action. I failed to get inspiration indoors or out; and feeling my health suffer from the constant irritation of my recurring disappointment, I resolved to take a day off and carry myself and my perplexities into the country.

I did so. Governed by an impulse which I did not then understand, I went to a small town in New Jersey and entered the first house on which I saw the sign "Room to Let." The result was most fortunate. No sooner had I crossed the threshold of the neat and homely apartment thrown open to my use, than it recalled a room in which I had slept two years before and in which I had read a little book I was only too glad to remember at this moment. Indeed, it seemed as if a veritable inspiration had come to me through this recollection, for though the tale to which I allude was a simple child's story written for moral purposes, it contained an idea which promised to be invaluable to me at this juncture. Indeed, by means of it, I believed myself to have solved the problem that was puzzling me, and relieved beyond expression, I paid for the night's lodging I had now determined to forego, and returned immediately to New York, having spent just fifteen minutes in the town where I had received this happy inspiration.

My first step on entering the city was to order a dozen steel coils made similar to the one which I still believed answerable for James Holmes' death. My next to learn as far as possible all of John Graham's haunts and habits. At a week's end I had the springs and knew almost as well as he did himself where he was likely to be found at all times of the day and night. I immediately acted upon this knowledge. Assuming a slight disguise, I repeated my former stroll through Printing-house Square, looking into each doorway as I passed. John Graham was in one of them, staring in his old way at the passing crowd, but evidently seeing nothing but the images formed by his own disordered brain. A manuscript-roll stuck out of his breast-pocket, and from the way his nervous fingers fumbled with it, I began to understand the restless glitter of his eyes, which were as full of wretchedness as any eyes I have ever seen.

Entering the doorway where he stood, I dropped at his feet one of the small steel coils with which I was provided. He did not see it. Stopping near him I directed his attention to it by saying:

"Pardon me, but did I not see something drop out of your hand?"

He started, glanced at the seeming inoffensive toy at which I pointed, and altered so suddenly and so vividly that it became instantly apparent that the surprise I had planned for him was fully as keen and searching a one as I had anticipated. Recoiling sharply, he gave me a quick look, then glanced down again at his feet as if half expecting to find the object vanished which had startled him. But, perceiving it still lying there, he crushed it viciously with his heel, and uttering some incoherent words, dashed impetuously from the building.

Confident that he would regret this hasty impulse and return, I withdrew a few steps and waited. And sure enough, in less than five minutes he came slinking back. Picking up the coil with more than one sly look about, he examined it closely. Suddenly he gave a sharp cry and went staggering out. Had he discovered that the seeming puzzle possessed the same invisible spring which had made the one handled by James Holmes so dangerous?

Certain as to the place he would be found in next, I made a short cut to an obscure little saloon in Nassau Street, where I took up my stand in a spot convenient for seeing without being seen. In ten minutes he was standing at the bar asking for a drink.

"Whiskey!" he cried, "straight."

It was given him; but as he set the empty glass down on the counter, he saw lying before him another of the steel springs, and was so confounded by the sight that the proprietor, who had put it there at my instigation, thrust out his hand toward him as if half afraid he would fall.

"Where did that—that *thing* come from?" stammered John Graham, ignoring the other's gesture and pointing with a trembling hand at the seemingly insignificant bit of wire between them.

"Didn't it drop from your coat-pocket?" inquired the proprietor. "It wasn't lying here before you came in."

With a horrible oath the unhappy man turned and fled from the place. I lost sight of him after that for three hours, then I suddenly came upon him again. He was walking up town with a set purpose in his face that made him look more dangerous than ever. Of course I followed him, expecting him to turn towards Fifty-ninth Street, but at the corner of Madison Avenue and Forty-seventh Street he changed his mind and dashed toward Third Avenue. At Park Avenue he faltered and again turned north, walking for several blocks as if the fiends were behind him. I began to think that he was but attempting to walk off his excitement, when, at a sudden rushing sound in the cut beside us, he stopped and trembled. An express train was shooting by. As it disappeared in the tunnel beyond, he looked about him with a blanched face and wandering eye; but his glance did not turn my way, or if it did, he failed to attach any meaning to my near presence.

He began to move on again and this time towards the bridge spanning the cut. I followed him very closely. In the center of it he paused and looked down at the track beneath him. Another train was approaching. As it came near he trembled from head to foot, and catching at the railing against which he leaned, was about to make a quick move forward when a puff of smoke arose from below and sent him staggering backward, gasping with a terror I could hardly understand till I saw that the smoke had taken the form of a spiral and was sailing away before him in what to his disordered imagination must have looked like a gigantic image of the coil with which twice before on this day he had found himself confronted.

It may have been chance and it may have been providence; but whichever it was it saved him. He could not face that semblance of his haunting thought; and turning away, he cowered down on the neighboring curbstone, where he sat for several minutes, with his head buried in his hands; when he rose again he was his own daring and sinister self. Knowing that he was now too much master of his faculties to ignore me any longer, I walked quickly away and left him. I knew where he would be at six o'clock and had already engaged a table at the same restaurant. It was seven, however, before he put in an appearance, and by this time he was looking more composed. There was a reckless air about him, however, which was perhaps only noticeable to me; for none of the habitues of this especial restaurant were entirely without it; wild eyes and unkempt hair being in the majority.

I let him eat. The dinner he ordered was simple and I had not the heart to interrupt his enjoyment of it.

But when he had finished, and came to pay, then I allowed the shock to come. Under the bill which the waiter laid at the side of his plate was the inevitable steel coil; and it produced even more than its usual effect. I own I felt sorry for him.

He did not dash from the place, however, as he had from the liquor-saloon. A spirit of resistance had seized him and he demanded to know where this object of his fear had come from. No one could tell him (or would). Whereupon he began to rave and would certainly have done himself or somebody else an injury if he had not been calmed by a man almost as wild-looking as himself. Paying his bill, but vowing he would never enter the place again, he went out, clay-white, but with the swaggering air of a man who had just asserted himself.

He drooped, however, as soon as he reached the street, and I had no difficulty in following him to a certain gambling den where he gained three dollars and lost five. From there he went to his lodgings in West Tenth Street.

I did not follow him in. He had passed through many deep and wearing emotions since noon, and I had not the heart to add another to them.

But late the next day I returned to this house and rang the bell. It was already dusk, but there was light enough for me to notice the unrepaired condition of the iron railings on either side of the old stone stoop and to compare this abode of decayed grandeur with the spacious and elegant apartment in which pretty Mrs. Holmes mourned the loss of her young husband. Had any such comparison ever been made by the unhappy John Graham, as he hurried up these decayed steps into the dismal halls beyond?

In answer to my summons there came to the door a young woman to whom I had but to intimate my wish to see Mr. Graham for her to let me in with the short announcement:

"Top floor, back room! Door open, he's out; door shut, he's in."

As an open door meant liberty to enter, I lost no time in following the direction of her pointing finger, and presently found myself in a low attic chamber overlooking an acre of roofs. A fire had been lighted in the open grate, and the flickering red beams danced on ceiling and walls with a cheeriness greatly in contrast to the nature of the business which had led me there. As they also served to light the room I proceeded to make myself at home; and drawing up a chair, sat down at the fireplace in such a way as to conceal myself from any one entering the door.

In less than half an hour he came in.

He was in a state of high emotion. His face was flushed and his eyes burning. Stepping rapidly forward, he flung his hat on the table in the middle of the room, with a curse that was half cry and half groan. Then he stood silent and I had an opportunity of noting how haggard he had grown in the short time which had elapsed since I had seen him last. But the interval of his inaction was short, and in a moment he flung up his arms with a loud "Curse her!" that rang through the narrow room and betrayed the source of his present frenzy. Then he again stood still, grating his teeth and working his hands in a way terribly suggestive of the murderer's instinct. But not for long. He saw something that attracted his attention on the table, a something upon which my eyes had long before been fixed, and starting forward with a fresh and quite different display of emotion, he caught up what looked like a roll of manuscript and began to tear it open.

"Back again! Always back!" wailed from his lips; and he gave the roll a toss that sent from its midst a small object which he no sooner saw than he became speechless and reeled back. It was another of the steel coils.

"Good God!" fell at last from his stiff and working lips. "Am I mad or has the devil joined in the pursuit against me? I cannot eat, I cannot drink, but this diabolical spring starts up before me. It is here, there, everywhere. The visible sign of my guilt; the—the——" He had stumbled back upon my chair, and turning, saw me.

I was on my feet at once, and noting that he was dazed by the shock of my presence, I slid quietly between him and the door.

The movement roused him. Turning upon me with a sarcastic smile in which was concentrated the bitterness of years, he briefly said:

"So, I am caught! Well, there has to be an end to men as well as to things, and I am ready for mine. She turned me away from her door to-day, and after the hell of that moment I don't much fear any other."

"You had better not talk," I admonished

him. “ All that falls from you now will only tell against you on your trial.”

He broke into a harsh laugh. “ And do you think I care for that? That having been driven by a woman’s perfidy into crime I am going to bridle my tongue and keep down the words which are my only safeguard from insanity? No, no; while my miserable breath lasts I will curse her, and if the halter is to cut short my words, it shall be with her name blistering my lips.”

I attempted to speak, but he would not give me the opportunity. The passion of weeks had found vent and he rushed on recklessly.

“ I went to her house to-day. I wanted to see her in her widow’s weeds; I wanted to see her eyes red with weeping over a grief which owed its bitterness to me. But she would not grant me an admittance. She had me thrust from her door, and I shall never know how deeply the iron has sunk into her soul. But —” and here his face showed a sudden change, “ I shall see her if I am tried for murder.

She will be in the court-room,—on the witness stand——"

"Doubtless," I interjected; but his interruption came quickly and with vehement passion.

"Then I am ready. Welcome trial, conviction, death, even. To confront her eye to eye is all I wish. She shall never forget it, never!"

"Then you do not deny——" I began.

"I deny nothing," he returned, and held out his hands with a grim gesture. "How can I, when there falls from everything I touch, the devilish thing which took away the life I hated?"

"Have you anything more to say or do before you leave these rooms?" I asked.

He shook his head, and then, bethinking himself, pointed to the roll of paper which he had flung on the table.

"Burn that!" he cried.

I took up the roll and looked at it. It was the manuscript of a poem in blank verse.

"I have been with it into a dozen newspaper and magazine offices," he explained with great bitterness. "Had I succeeded in getting a publisher for it I might have forgotten my wrongs and tried to build up a new life on the ruins of the old. But they would not have it, none of them, so I say, burn it! that no memory of me may remain in this miserable world."

"Keep to the facts!" I severely retorted. "It was while carrying this poem from one newspaper to another that you secured that bit of print upon the blank side of which you yourself printed the obituary notice with which you savored your revenge upon the woman who had disappointed you."

"You know that? Then you know where I got the poison with which I tipped the silly toy with which that weak man fooled away his life?"

"No," said I, "I do not know where you got it. I merely know it was no common poison bought at a druggist's, or from any ordinary chemist."

"It was woorali; the deadly, secret woorali. I got it from—but that is another man's secret. You will never hear from me anything that will compromise a friend. I got it, that is all. One drop, but it killed my man."

The satisfaction, the delight, which he threw into these words are beyond description. As they left his lips a jet of flame from the neglected fire shot up and threw his figure for one instant into bold relief upon the lowering ceiling; then it died out, and nothing but the twilight dusk remained in the room and on the countenance of this doomed and despairing man.

THE GRAY MADAM

THE GRAY MADAM.[1]

WAS it a specter?

For days I could not answer this question. I am no believer in spiritual manifestations, yet— But let me tell my story.

I was lodging with my wife on the first floor of a house in Twenty-seventh street. I had taken the apartments for three months, and we had already lived in them two and found them sufficiently comfortable. The back room we used as a bedroom, and while it communicated with the hall, we invariably made use of the front parlor-door to go in and out of. Two great leaves of old mahogany connected the two rooms, and as we received but few friends, these doors usually stood half open.

One morning, my wife being ill, I left her

lying in bed and stepped into the parlor preparatory to going out for breakfast. It was late—nine o'clock, probably—and I was hastening to leave, when I heard a sound behind me—or did I merely feel a presence?—and, turning, saw a strange and totally unknown woman coming toward me from my wife's room.

As I had just left that room, and as there was no way of getting into it except through a door we always kept locked, I was so overpowered by my astonishment that I never thought of speaking or moving until she had passed me. Then I found voice, and calling out " Madam! " endeavored to stop her.

But the madam, if madam she was, passed on as quietly, as mechanically even, as if I had not raised my voice, and, before I could grasp the fact that she was melting from before me, flitted through the hall to the front door and so out, leaving behind on the palm of my hand the " feel " of her wool dress, which I had just managed to touch.

Not understanding her or myself or the strange thrill awakened by this contact, I tore open the front door and looked out, expecting, of course, to see her on the steps or on the sidewalk in front. But there was no one of her appearance visible, and I came back questioning whether I was the victim of a hallucination or just an everyday fool. To satisfy myself on this important question I looked about for the hall-boy, with the intention of asking him if he had seen any such person go out, but that young and inconsequent scamp was missing from his post as usual, and there was no one within sight to appeal to.

There was nothing to do but to re-enter my rooms, where my attention was immediately arrested by the sight of my wife sitting up in bed and surveying me with a look of unmistakable astonishment.

"Who was that woman?" she asked. "And how came she in here?"

So she had seen her too.

"What woman, Lydia? I have not let in any woman. Did you think there was a woman in this room?"

"Not in that room," she answered hoarsely, "but in this one. I saw her just now passing through the folding doors. Wilbur, I am frightened. See how my hands shake. Do you think I am sick enough to imagine things?"

I knew she was not, but I did not say so. I thought it would be better for her to think herself under some such delusion.

"You were dozing," said I. "If you had seen a woman here, you could tell me how she looked."

"And I can," my wife broke in excitedly. "She was like the ghosts we read of, only that her dress and the veil or drapery she wore were all gray. Didn't you see her? You must have seen her. She went right by you—a gray woman, all gray; a lady, Wilbur, and slightly lame. Could I have dreamed all that?"

"You must have!" I cried, shaking the one door communicating with the hall, so she might see it was locked, and even showing her the key of it, lying in its accustomed place behind the bureau cushion. Yet I was in no satisfied condition myself, for she had described with the greatest accuracy the very person I had myself seen. Had we been alike the victims of a spiritual manifestation?

This was Tuesday. On Friday my question seemed to receive an answer. I had been down town, as usual, and on returning found a crowd assembled in front of my lodging-house. A woman had been run over and was being carried into our rooms. In the glimpse I caught of her I saw that she was middle-aged and was wrapped in a long black cloak. Later, this cloak fell off, as her hat had done long before, and I perceived that her dress was black and decent.

She was laid on our bed and every attention paid her. But she had been grievously injured about the head and gradually but surely sank before our eyes. Suddenly she roused and gave a look about her. It was a remarkable one—a look of recognition and almost of delight. Then she raised one hand and, pointing with a significant gesture into the empty space before her, sank back and died.

It was a sudden ending, and, anxious to see its effect upon my wife, who was standing on the other side of the bed, I glanced her way with some misgiving. She showed more feeling than I had anticipated. Indeed her countenance was a study, and when, under, the influence of my scrutiny she glanced my way, I saw that something of deeper import than this unexpected death in our rooms lay at the bottom of her uneasy look.

What that was, I was soon to know, for catching up from amid the folds of the woman's gray-lined cloak a long gray veil which had fallen at the bedside, she disposed it softly about the woman's face, darting me a look full of significance.

"You remember the vision I had the morning when I was sick?" she whispered softly in my ear.

I nodded, secretly thrilled to my very heart's core.

"Well, it was a vision of this woman. If she were living and on her feet and wrapped, as I have shown you, in this veil, you would behold a living picture of the person I saw passing out of this room that morning."

"I shall not dispute you," I answered. Alas, I had myself perceived the likeness the minute the veil had fallen about the pinched but handsome features!

"A forewarning," whispered my wife, "a forewarning of what has this day happened under our roof. It was a wraith we saw. Wilbur, I shall not spend another night in these rooms."

And we did not. I was as anxious to leave as she was. Yet I am not a superstitious man. As proof of it, after the first effect of these events had left me, I began to question my first impressions and feel tolerably ashamed of my past credulity. Though the phenomenon we had observed could not to all appearance be explained by any natural hypothesis; though I had seen, and my wife had seen, a strange woman suddenly become visible in a room which a moment before had held no one but ourselves, and into which no live woman could have entered without our knowledge, something —was it my natural good sense?—recoiled before a supernatural explanation of this, and I found myself forced to believe that our first visitor had been as real as the last; in other words, the same woman.

But could I prove it? Could the seemingly impossible be made possible and the unexplainable receive a solution satisfying to a rational mind? I determined to make an effort to accomplish this, if only to relieve the mind of my wife, who had not recovered her equanimity as readily as myself.

Starting with the assumption above mentioned—that the woman who had died in our presence was the same who had previously found an unexplainable entrance into these same rooms—I first inquired if the black cloak lined with gray did not offer a solution to some of my previous difficulties. It was a long cloak, enveloping her completely. When worn with the black side out, she would present an inconspicuous appearance, but with the gray side out and the effect of this heightened by a long gray veil flung over her hat, she would look like the gray lady I had first seen. Now, a cloak can be turned in an instant, and if she had chosen to do this in flitting through my door I would naturally find only a sedate, black-clothed woman passing up the street, when, rousing from the apathy into which her appearance had thrown me, I rushed to the front door and looked out. Had I seen such a woman? I seemed to remember that I had.

Thus much, then, was satisfactory, but to account for her entrance into our rooms was not so easy. Had she slipped by me in coming in as she had on going out? The parlor door was open, for I had been out to get the paper. Could she have glided in by me unperceived and thus have found her way into the bedroom from which I afterward saw her issue? No, for I had stood facing the front hall door all the time. Through the bedroom door then? But that was, as I have said, locked. Here was a mystery, then; but it was one worth solving.

My first step was to recall all that I had heard of the actual woman who had been buried from our rooms. Her name, as ascertained in the cheap boarding-house to which she was traced, was Helmuth, and she was, so far as any one knew, without friends or relatives in the city. To those who saw her daily she was a harmless, slightly demented woman with money enough to live above want, but not enough to warrant her boasting talk about the rich things she was going to buy some day and the beautiful presents she would soon be in a position to give away. The money found on her person was sufficient to bury her, but no papers were in her possession, nor an letters calculated to throw light upon her past life.

Her lameness had been caused by paralysis, but the date of her attack was not known.

Finding no clue in this to what I wished to learn, I went back to our old rooms, which had not been let since our departure, and sought for one there, and, strangely enough, I found it. I thought I knew everything there was to be known about the apartment we had lived in two months, but one little fact had escaped me which, under the scrutiny that I now gave it, became apparent. This was simply that the key which opened the hall door of the bedroom and which we had seldom if ever used was not as old a key as that of the corresponding door in the parlor, and this fact, small as it was, led me to make inquiries.

The result was that I learned something about the couple who had preceded us in the use of these rooms. They were of middle age and of great personal elegance, but uncertain pay, the husband being nothing more nor less than a professional gambler. Their name was L'Hommedieu.

When I first heard of them, I thought that Mrs. L'Hommedieu might be the Mrs. Helmuth in whose history I was so interested, but from all I could learn she was a very different sort of person. Mrs. L'Hommedieu was gay, dashing and capable of making a show out of a flimsy silk a shop-girl would hesitate to wear. Yet she looked distinguished and wore her cheap jewelry with more grace than many a woman her diamonds. I would, consequently, have dropped this inquiry if some one had not remarked upon her having had a paralytic stroke after leaving the house. This, together with the fact that the key to the rear door, which I had found replaced by a new one, had been taken away by her and never returned, connected her so indubitably with my mysterious visitor that I resolved to pursue my investigations into Mrs. L'Hommedieu's past.

For this purpose I sought out a quaint little maiden-lady living on the top floor, who, I was told, knew more about the L'Hommedieus than any one in the building. Miss Winterburn, whose acquaintance I had failed to make while residing in the house, was a fluttering, eager, affable person, whose one delight was, as I soon found, to talk about the L'Hommedieus. Of the story she related I give as much as I can of it in her own words.

"I was never their equal," said she, "but Mrs. L'Hommedieu was lonely, and, having no friends in town, was good enough to admit me to her parlor now and then and even to allow me to accompany her to the theater when her husband was away on one of his mysterious visits. I never liked Mr. L'Hommedieu, but I did like her. She was so different from me, and, when I first knew her, so gay and so full of conversation. But after awhile she changed and was either feverishly cheerful or morbidly sad, so that my visits caused me more pain than pleasure. The reason for these changes in her was patent to everybody. Though her husband was a handsome man, he was as unprincipled as he was unfortunate. He gambled. This she once admitted to me, and while at long intervals he met with some luck he more often returned dispirited and with that hungry, ravening look you expect to see in a wolf cheated of its prey.

"I used to be afraid he would strike her after some one of these disappointments, but I do not think he ever did. She had a determined character of her own, and there have been times when I have thought he was as much afraid of her as she was of him. I became sure of this after one night. Mrs. L'Hommedieu and myself were having a little supper together in the front parlor you have so lately occupied. It was a very ordinary supper, for the L'Hommedieus' purse had run low, and Mrs. L'Hommedieu was not the woman to spend much at any time on her eating. It was palatable, however, and had been cooked by us both together, and I was enjoying it and would have enjoyed it more if Mrs. L'Hommedieu had had more appetite. But she ate scarcely anything and seemed very anxious and unhappy, though she laughed now and then with sudden gusts of mirth too hysterical to be real. It was not late, and yet we were both very much surprised when there came a knock at the door, followed by the entrance of a visitor.

"Mrs. L'Hommedieu, who is always *la grande dame*, rose without apparent embarrassment to meet the gentleman who entered, though I knew she could not help but feel keenly the niggardly appearance of the board she left with such grace. The stranger—he was certainly a stranger; this I could see by the formality of her manner—was a gentleman of urbane bearing and a general air of prosperity.

"I remember every word that passed.

"'My name is Lafarge,' said he. 'I am, or rather have been, under great obligations to your husband, and I have come to discharge my debt. Is he at home?'

"Mrs. L'Hommedieu's eye, which had sparkled at his name, dropped suddenly as he put the final question.

"'I am sorry,' she returned after a moment of embarrassment, 'but my husband is very seldom home evenings. If you could come about noon some day'—

"'Thank you,' said he, with a bright smile, 'but I will finish my business now and with you, seeing that Mr. L'Hommedieu is not at home. Years ago—I am sure you have heard your husband mention my name—I borrowed quite a sum of money from him, which I have never paid. You recall the amount, no doubt?'

"'I have heard Mr. L'Hommedieu say it was a thousand dollars,' she replied, with a sudden fluttering of her hands indicative of great excitement.

"'That is the sum,' he allowed, either not noticing me or thinking me too insignificant to be considered. 'I regret to have kept him so long out of it, but I have not forgotten to add the interest in making out this statement of my indebtedness, and if you will look over this paper and acknowledge its correctness I will leave the equivalent of my debt here and now, for I sail for Europe to-morrow morning and wish to have all my affairs in order before leaving.'

"Mrs. L'Hommedieu, who looked ready to faint from excess of feeling, summoned up her whole strength, looking so beautiful as she did so, that one forgot the ribbons on her sleeves were no longer fresh and that the silk dress she wore hung in the very limpest of folds.

"'I am obliged to you,' she said in a tone from which she strove in vain to suppress all eagerness. 'And if I may speak for Mr. L'Hommedieu he will be as grateful for your remembrance of us as for the money you so kindly offer to return to him.'

"The stranger bowed low and took out a folded paper, which he handed her. He was not deceived, I am sure, by her grand airs, and knew as well as I did that no woman ever stood in greater need of money. But nothing in his manner betrayed this knowledge.

"'It is a bond I give you,' he now explained. 'As you will see, it has coupons attached to it, which you can cash at any time. It will prove as valuable to you as so much ready money and possibly more convenient.'

"And with just this hint, which I took as significant of his complete understanding of her position, he took her receipt and politely left the house.

"Once alone with me who am nobody, her joy had full vent. I have never seen any one so lost in delight as she was for a few minutes. To have this money thrust upon her just at a moment when actual want seemed staring her in the face was too much of a relief for her to conceal either the misery she had been under or the satisfaction she now enjoyed. Under the gush of her emotions her whole history came out, but as you have often heard the like I will not repeat it, especially as it was all contained in the cry with which a little later she thrust the bond toward me.

"'He must not see it! He must not! It would go like all the rest, and I would again be left without a cent. Take it and keep it, for I have no means of concealing it here. He is too suspicious.'

"But this was asking more than I was willing to grant. Seeing how I felt, she thrust the paper into her bosom with a look before which I secretly recoiled. 'You will not charge yourself with such a responsibility?' said she. 'But I can trust you not to tell him?'

"'Yes,' I nodded, feeling sick of the whole business.

"'Then'— But here the door was violently flung open and without any warning Mr. L'Hommedieu burst into the room in a state of as much excitement as his wife, only his was the excitement of desperation.

"'Gone! Gone!' he cried, ignoring me as completely as had Mr. Lafarge. 'Not a dollar left; not even my studs! See!' And he pointed to his shirt front hanging apart in a way I would never have looked for in this reckless but fastidious gentleman. 'Yet if I had had a dollar more or even a ring worth a dollar or so I might have— Theresa, have you any money at all? A coin now might save us.'

"Mrs. L'Hommedieu, who had turned alarmingly pale, drew up her fine figure and resolutely confronted him. 'No!' said she, and shifting her gaze she turned it meaningly upon me.

"He misunderstood this movement. Thinking it simply a reminder of my presence, he turned and, with his false but impressive show of courtesy, made me a low bow. Then he forgot me utterly again, and facing his wife, growled out:

"'Where are you going to get breakfast then? You don't look like a woman who expects to starve!'

"It was a fatal remark, for, do what she would, she could not prevent a slight smile of disdain, and, seeing it, he kept his eyes riveted on her face till her uneasiness became manifest. Instantly his suspicion took form, and, surveying her still more fixedly, he espied a corner of the precious paper protruding slightly above her corsage. To snatch it out, open it and realize its value was the work of a moment. Her cry of dismay and his shout of mad triumph rang out simultaneously, and never have I seen such an ebullition of opposing passions as I was made witness to as his hand closed over this small fortune and their staring eyes met in the mortal struggle they had now entered upon for its ultimate possession.

"She was the first to speak. 'It was given to me; it was meant for me. If I keep it, both of us will profit by it, but if you——'

"He did not wait for her to finish. 'Where did you get it?' he cried. 'I can break the bank with what I can raise on this bond at the club. Darraugh's in town. You know what that means. Luck's in the air, and with an hundred dollars— But I've no time to talk. I came for a dollar, a fifty-cent piece, a dime even, and I go back with a bond worth——'

"But she was already between him and the door. 'You will never carry that bond out of this house,' she whispered in the tone which goes further than any cry. 'I have not held it in my hand to see it follow every other good thing I have had in life. I will not, Henry. Take that bond and sink it as you have all the rest and I fall at your feet a dead woman. I will never survive the destruction of my last hope.'

"He was cowed—for a moment, that is; she looked so superb and so determined. Then all that was mean and despicable in his thinly veneered nature came to the surface, and, springing forward with an oath, he was about to push her aside, when, without the moving of a finger on her part, he reeled back, recovered himself, caught at a chair, missed it and fell heavily to the floor.

"'My God, I thank thee!' was the exclamation with which she broke from the trance of terror into which she had been thrown by his sudden attempt to pass her; and without a glance at his face, which to me looked like the face of a dead man, she tore the paper from his hand and stood looking about her with a wild and searching gaze, in the desperate hope that somehow the walls would open and offer her a safe place of concealment for the precious sheet of paper.

Meanwhile I had crept near the prostrate man. He was breathing, but was perfectly unconscious.

"'Don't you mean to do something for him?' I asked. 'He may die.'

"She met my question with the dazed air of one suddenly awakened. 'No, he'll not die, but he'll not come to for some minutes, and this must be hidden first. But where? where? I cannot trust it on my person or in any place a man like him would search. I must devise some means—ah!'

"With this final exclamation she had dashed into the other room. I did not see where she went—I did not want to—but I soon realized she was working somewhere in a desperate hurry. I could hear her breath coming in quick, short pants as I bent over her husband, waiting for him to rouse and hating my inaction even while I succumbed to it.

"Suddenly she was back in the parlor again, and to my surprise passed immediately to the little table in the corner where we had sat at supper. We had had for our simple refreshment that homeliest of all dishes, boiled milk thickened with flour. There was still some left in a bowl, and taking this away with her, she called back hoarsely:

"'Pray that he does not come to till I have finished. It will be the best prayer you ever made.'

"She told me afterward that he was subject to these attacks and that she had long ceased to be alarmed by them. But to me the sight of this man lying there so helpless, was horrible and, though I hated him and pitied her, I scarcely knew what to wish. While battling with my desire to run and the feeling of loyalty which held me kneeling at that man's side, I heard her speak again, this time in an even and slightly hard tone: 'Now you may dash a glass of cold water in his face. I am prepared to meet him. Happily his memory fails him after these attacks. I may succeed in making him believe that the bond he saw was one of his fancies.'

"'Had you not better throw the water yourself?' I suggested, getting up and meeting her eye very quietly.

"She looked at me in wonder, then moved calmly to the table, took the glass and dashed a few drops of water into her husband's face. Instantly he began to stir, seeing which I arose without haste, but without any unnecessary delay, and quietly took my leave. I could bear no more that night.

"Next morning I awoke in a fright. I had dreamed that he had come to my room in search of the bond. But it was only her knock at the door and her voice, asking if she might enter at this early hour. It was such a relief I gladly let her in, and she entered with her best air and flung herself on my little lounge with the hysterical cry:

"'He has sent me up. I told him I ought not to intrude at such an inconvenient hour;

that you would not have had your breakfast.' (How carelessly she spoke! How hard she tried to keep the hungry note out of her voice!) 'But he insisted upon my coming up. I know why. He searched me before I left the room, and now he wants to search the room itself.'

"'Then he did remember?' I began.

"'Yes, he remembers now. I saw it in his eyes as soon as he awoke. But he will not find the bond. That is safe, and some day when I shall have escaped his vigilance long enough to get it back again I will use it so as to make him as well as myself comfortable. I am not a selfish woman.'

"I did not think she was, and I felt pity for her, and so after dressing and making her a cup of tea—I can myself do very well without one on a pinch—I sat down with her, and we chatted for an hour or so quite comfortably. Then she grew so restless and consulted the clock so often that I tried to soothe her by remarking that it was not an easy task he had set himself, at which she laughed in a mysterious way, but failed to grow less anxious till our suspense was cut short by the appearance of the janitor with a message from Mr. L'Hommedieu.

"'Mr. L'Hommedieu's compliments,' said he, 'and he hopes Mrs. L'Hommedieu will make herself comfortable and not think of coming down. He is doing everything that is necessary and will soon be through. You can rest quite easy, ma'am.'

"'What does he mean?' marveled the poor woman as the janitor disappeared. 'Is he spending all this time ransacking the rooms? I wish I dared disobey him. I wish I dared go down.'

"But her courage was not equal to an open disregard of his wishes, and she had to subdue her impatience and wait for a summons that did not come till near two o'clock. Then Mr. L'Hommedieu himself appeared with her hat and mantle on his arm.

"'My dear,' said he as she rose, haggard

with excitement, to meet him, 'I have brought your wraps with me that you may go directly from here to our new home. Shall I assist you to put them on? You do not look as well as usual, and that is why I have undertaken this thing all myself—to save you, my dear; to save you each and every exertion.'

"I had flung out my arms to catch her, for I thought she was going to faint, but she did not, though I think it would have been better for her if she had.

"'We are going to leave this house?' she asked, speaking very slowly and with a studied lack of emotion that imposed upon nobody.

"'I have said so,' he smiled. 'The dray has already taken away the half of our effects, and the rest will follow at Mrs. Latimer's convenience.'

"'Ah, I understand!' she replied, with a gasp of relief significant of her fear that by some superhuman cunning he had found the bond she thought so safely concealed. 'I was wondering how Mrs. Latimer came to allow us to leave.' (I tell you they always talked as if I were not present.) 'Our goods are left as a surety, it seems.'

"'Half of our goods,' he blandly corrected. 'Would it interest you to know which half?'

"'The cunning of this insinuation was matched by the imperturbable shrug with which she replied. 'So a bed has been allowed us and some clothes I am satisfied,' at which he bit his lips, vexed at her self-control and his own failure to break it.

"'You have not asked where we are going,' he observed as with apparent solicitude he threw her mantle over her shoulders.

"The air of lassitude with which she replied bespoke her feeling on that point. 'I have little curiosity,' she said. 'You know I can be happy anywhere. And, turning toward me, she moved her lips in a way I interpreted to mean: 'Go below with me. See me out.'

"'Say what you have to say to Miss Winterburn aloud,' he dryly suggested.

"'I have nothing to say to Miss Winterburn

but thanks,' was her cold reply, belied, however, by the trembling of her fingers as she essayed to fit on her gloves.

"'And those I will receive below!' I cried, with affected gaiety. 'I am going down with you to the door.' And resolutely ignoring his frown I tripped down before them. On the last stair I felt her steps lagging. Instantly I seemed to comprehend what was required of me, and, rushing forward, I entered the front parlor. He followed close behind me, for how could he know I was not in collusion with her to regain the bond? This gave her one minute by herself in the rear, and in that minute she secured the key which would give her future access to the spot where her treasure lay hidden.

"The rest of the story I must give you mainly from hearsay. You must understand by this time what Mr. L'Hommedieu's scheme was in moving thus suddenly. He knew that it would be impossible for him, by the most minute and continuous watchfulness, to prevent his wife from recovering the bond while they continued to inhabit the rooms in which, notwithstanding his failure to find it, he had reason to believe it still lay concealed. But once in other quarters it would be comparatively easy for him to subject her to a surveillance which not only would prevent her from returning to this house without his knowledge, but would lead her to give away her secret by the very natural necessity she would be under of going to the exact spot where her treasure lay hid.

"It was a cunning plot and showed him to be as able as he was unscrupulous. How it worked I will now proceed to tell you. It must have been the next afternoon that the janitor came running up to me—I suppose he had learned by this time that I had more than ordinary interest in these people—to say that Mrs. L'Hommedieu had been in the house and had been so frightened by a man who had followed her that she had fainted dead away on the floor. Would I go down to her?

"I had rather have gone anywhere else, unless it was to prison, but duty cannot be shirked, and I followed the man down. But we were too late. Mrs. L'Hommedieu had recovered and gone away, and the person who had frightened her was also gone, and only the hall-boy remained to give any explanations.

"This was what he had to say:

"'The man it was who went first. As soon as the lady fell he skipped out. I don't think he meant no good here——'

"'Did she drop here in the hall?' I asked, unable to restrain my intense anxiety.

"'Oh, no, ma'am! They was in the back room yonder, which she got in somehow. The man followed her in, sneaking and sneaking like an eel or a cop, and she fell right against——'

"'Don't tell me where!' I cried. 'I don't want to know where!' And I was about to return up-stairs when I heard a quick, sharp voice behind me and realized that Mr. L'Hommedieu had come in and was having some dispute with the janitor.

"Common prudence led me to listen. He wanted, as was very natural, to enter the room where his wife had just been surprised, but the janitor, alarmed by the foregoing very irregular proceedings, was disposed to deny his right to do so.

"'The furniture is held as a surety,' said he, 'and I have orders——'

"But Mr. L'Hommedieu had a spare dollar, and before many minutes had elapsed I heard him go into that room and close the door. Of the next ten minutes and the suspense I felt I need not speak. When he came out again, he looked as if the ground would not hold him.

"'I have done some mischief, I fear,' he airily said as he passed by the janitor. 'But I'll pay for it. Don't worry. I'll pay for it and the rent, too, to-morrow. You may tell Mrs. Latimer so.' And he was gone, leaving us all agape in the hallway.

"A minute later we all crept to that room

and looked in. Now that he had got the money I for one was determined to know where she had hid it. There was no mistaking the spot. A single glance was enough to show us the paper ripped off from a portion of the wall, revealing a narrow gap behind the base-board large enough to hold the bond. It was near——"

"Wait!" I put in as I remembered where the so called Mrs. Helmuth had pointed just before she died. "Wasn't it at the left of the large folding doors and midway to the wall?"

"How came you to know?" she asked. "Did Mrs. Latimer tell you?" But as I did not answer she soon took up the thread of her narrative again, and, sighing softly, said:

"The next day came and went, but no Mr. L'Hommedieu appeared; another, and I be-gan to grow seriously uneasy; a third, and a dreadful thing happened. Late in the after-noon Mrs. L'Hommedieu, dressed very oddly for her, came sliding in at the front door, and with an appealing smile at the hall-boy, who wished but dared not ask her for the key which made these visits possible, glided by to her old rooms, and, finding the door unlocked, went softly in. Her appearance is worth description, for it shows the pitiful efforts she made at disguise, in the hope, I suppose, of escaping the surveillance she was evidently conscious of being under. She was in the habit of wearing on cool days a black circular with a gray lining. This she had turned inside out so that the gray was uppermost, while over her neat black bonnet she had flung a long veil, also gray, which not only hid her face, but gave to her appearance an eccentric look as different as possible from her usual aspect. The hall-boy, who had never seen her save in showy black or bright colors, said she looked like a ghost in the daytime, but it was all done for a purpose, I am sure, and to escape the attention of the man who had before followed her. Alas, he might have followed her this time without addition to her suffering! Scarcely had she entered the room where her treasure had been left than she saw the torn paper and gaping baseboard, and, uttering a cry so piercing it found its way even to the stolid heart of the hall-boy, she tottered back into the hall, where she fell into the arms of her husband, who had followed her in from the street in a state of frenzy almost equal to her own.

"The janitor, who that minute appeared on the stairway, says that he never saw two such faces. They looked at each other and were speechless. He was the first to hang his head.

"'It is gone, Henry,' she whispered. 'It is gone. You have taken it.'

"He did not answer.

"'And it is lost! You have risked it, and it is lost!'

"He uttered a groan. 'You should have given it to me that night. There was luck in the air then. Now the devil is in the cards and—'

"Her arms went up with a shriek. 'My curse be upon you, Henry L'Hommedieu!' And whether it was the look with which she said this that moved him, or whether there was some latent love in his heart for this once beautiful and long-suffering woman, he shrank at her words, and, stumbling like a man in the darkness, uttered a heart-rending groan and rushed from the house. We never saw him again.

" As for her, she fell this time under a paralytic attack which robbed her of her faculties. She was taken to a hospital, where I frequently visited her, but either from grief or the effect of her attack she did not know me, nor did she ever recognize any of us again. Mrs. Latimer, who is a just woman, sold her furniture and after paying herself out of the proceeds, gave the remainder to the hospital nurses in charge for Mrs. L'Hommedieu, so that when she left there she had something with which to start life anew. But where she went or how she managed to get along in her enfeebled condition I do not know. I never heard of her again."

" Then you did not see the woman who died in those rooms ? " I asked.

The effect of these words was magical and led to mutual explanations. She had not seen that woman, having encountered all the sorrow she wished to in that room. Nor was there any one else in the house who would be likely to recognize Mrs. L'Hommedieu ; both the janitor and hall-boy being new and Mrs. Latimer one of those proprietors who are only seen on rent day. For the rest, Mrs. L'Hommedieu's defective memory, which had led her to haunt the house and room where her money had once been hidden, accounted not only for her first visit, but the last, which had ended so fatally. The cunning she showed in turning her cloak and flinging a veil over her hat was the cunning of a partially clouded mind. It was a reminiscence of the morning when her terrible misfortune occurred. My habit of taking the key out of the lock of that unused door made the use of her own key possible, and her fear of being followed, caused her to lock the door behind her. My wife, who must have fallen into a doze on my leaving her, did not see her enter, but detected her just as she was trying to escape through the folding doors. My presence in the parlor probably added to her embarrassment, and she fled, turning her cloak as she did so.

How simple it seemed now that we knew the facts; but how obscure, and to all appearance, unexplainable, before the clew was given to the mystery!

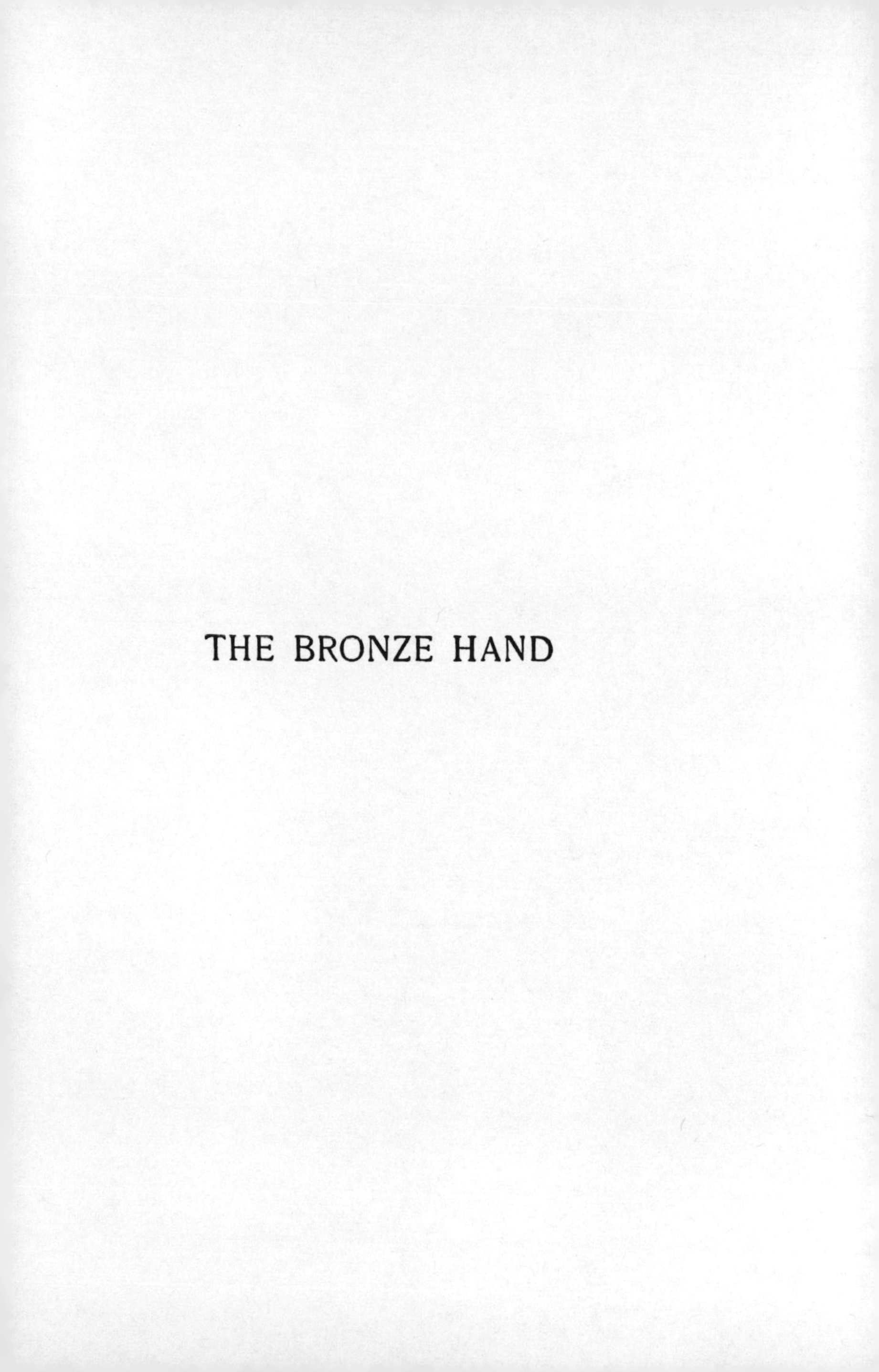

THE BRONZE HAND

THE BRONZE HAND.[1]

I.

THE FASCINATING UNKNOWN.

HER room was on the ground floor of the house we mutually inhabited, and mine directly above it, so that my opportunities for seeing her were limited to short glimpses of her auburn head as she leaned out of the window to close her shutters at night or open them in the morning. Yet our chance encounter in the hall or on the walk in front, had made so deep an impression upon my sensibilities that I was never without the vision of her pale face set off by the aureole of reddish brown hair, which, since my first meeting with her, had become for me the symbol of everything beautiful, incomprehensible and strange.

For my fellow-lodger was a mystery.

I am a busy man now, but just at the time of which I speak, I had leisure in abundance.

I was sharing with many others the unrest of the perilous days subsequent to the raid of John Brown at Harper's Ferry. Abraham Lincoln had been elected President. Baltimore, where the incidents I am relating transpired, had become the headquarters of men who secretly leagued themselves in antagonism to the North. Men and women who felt that their Northern brethren had grievously wronged them planned to undermine the stability of the government. The schemes at this time were gigantic in their conception and far-reaching in their scope and endless ramifications.

Naturally under these conditions, a consciousness of ever-present danger haunted every thinking mind. The candor of the outspoken was regarded with doubt, and the reticence of the more cautious, with distrust. It was a trying time for sensitive, impressionable natures with nothing to do. Perhaps all this may account for the persistency with which I sat in my open window. I was thus sitting one night --a memorable one to me—when I heard a sharp exclamation from below, in a voice I had long listened for.

Any utterance from those lips would have attracted my attention ; but, filled as this was with marked, if not extraordinary, emotion, I could not fail to be roused to a corresponding degree of curiosity and interest.

Thrusting out my head, I cast a rapid glance downward. A shutter swinging in the wind, and the escaping figure of a man hurrying round the corner of the street, were all that rewarded my scrutiny ; though, from the stream of light issuing from the casement beneath, I perceived that her window, like my own, was wide open.

As I continued to watch this light, I saw her thrust out her head with an eagerness indicative of great excitement. Peering to right and left, she murmured some suppressed words mixed with gasps of such strong feeling that I involuntarily called out:

"Excuse me, madam, have you been frightened in any way by the man I saw running away from here a moment ago?"

She gave a great start and glanced up. I see her face yet—beautiful, wonderful; so beautiful and so wonderful I have never been able to forget it. Meeting my eye, she faltered out:

"Did you see a man running away from here? Oh, sir, if I might have a word with you!"

I came near leaping directly to the pavement in my ardor and anxiety to oblige her, but, remembering before it was too late that she was neither a Juliet nor I a Romeo, I merely answered that I would be with her in a moment and betook myself below by the less direct but safer means of the staircase.

It was a short one and I was but a moment in descending, but that moment was long enough for my heart to acquire a most uncomfortable throb, and it was with anything but an air of quiet self-possession that I approached the threshold I had never before dared to cross even in fancy.

The door was open and I caught one glimpse of her figure before she was aware of my presence. She was contemplating her right hand with a look of terror, which, added to her striking personality, made her seem at the instant a creature of alarming characteristics fully as capable of awakening awe as devotion.

I may have given some token of the agitation her appearance awakened, for she turned towards me with sudden vehemence.

"Oh!" she cried, with a welcoming gesture; "you are the gentleman from up-stairs who saw a man running away from here a moment ago. Would you know that man if you saw him again?"

"I am afraid not," I replied. "He was only a flying figure in my eyes."

"Oh!" she moaned, bringing her hands together in dismay. But, immediately straightening herself, she met my regard with one as direct as my own. "I need a friend," she said, "and I am surrounded by strangers."

I made a move towards her; I did not feel myself a stranger. But how was I to make her realize the fact?

"If there is anything I can do," I suggested.

Her steady regard became searching.

"I have noticed you before to-night," she declared, with a directness devoid of every vestige of coquetry. "You seem to have qualities that may be trusted. But the man capable of helping me needs the strongest motives that influence humanity: courage, devotion, discretion, and a total forgetfulness of self. Such qualifications cannot be looked for in a stranger."

As if with these words she dismissed me from her thoughts, she turned her back upon me. Then, as if recollecting the courtesy due even to strangers, she cast me an apologetic glance over her shoulder and hurriedly added:

"I am bewildered by my loss. Leave me to

the torment of my thoughts. You can do nothing for me."

Had there been the least evidence of falsity in her tone or the slightest striving after effect in her look or bearing, I would have taken her at her word and left her then and there. But the candor of the woman and the reality of her emotion were not to be questioned, and moved by an impulse as irresistible as it was foolhardy, I cried with the impetuosity of my twenty-one years :

" I am ready to risk my life for you. Why, I do not know and do not care to ask. I only know you could have found no other man so willing to do your bidding."

A smile, in which surprise was tempered by a feeling almost tender, crossed her lips and immediately vanished. She shook her head as if in deprecation of the passion my words evinced, and was about to dismiss me, when she suddenly changed her mind and seized upon the aid I had offered, with a fervor that roused my sense of chivalry and deepened what might have been but a passing fancy into an active and all-engrossing passion.

"I can read faces," said she, "and I have read yours. You will do for me what I cannot do for myself, but——Have you a mother living?"

I answered no; that I was very nearly without relatives or ties.

"I am glad," she said, half to herself. Then with a last searching look, "Have you not even a sweetheart?"

I must have reddened painfully, for she drew back with a hesitating and troubled air; but the vigorous protest I hastened to make seemed to reassure her, for the next word she uttered was one of confidence.

"I have lost a ring." She spoke in a low but hurried tone. "It was snatched from my finger as I reached out my hand to close my shutters. Some one must have been lying in wait; some one who knows my habits and the hour at which I close my window for the night. The loss I have sustained is greater than you can conceive. It means more, much more, than appears. To the man who will bring me back that ring direct from the hand that stole it, I would devote the gratitude of a lifetime. Are you willing to make the endeavor? It is a task I cannot give to the police."

This request, so different from any I had expected, checked my enthusiasm in proportion as it awoke a senseless jealousy.

"Yet it seems directly in their line," I suggested, seeing nothing but humiliation before me if I attempted the recovery of a simple love-token.

"I know that it must seem so to you," she admitted, reading my thoughts and answering them with skilful indirectness. "But what policeman would undertake a difficult and minute search for an article whose intrinsic value would not reach five dollars?"

"Then it is only a memento," I stammered, with very evident feeling.

"Only a memento," she repeated; "but not of love. Worthless as it is in itself, it would buy everything I possess, and almost my soul to-night. I can explain no further. Will you attempt its recovery ?"

Restored to myself by her frank admission that it was no lover's keepsake I was urged to recapture and return, I allowed the powerful individuality of this woman to have its full effect upon me. Taking in with one glance her beauty, the impassioned fervor of her nature, and the subtle charm of a spirit she now allowed to work its full spell upon me, I threw every practical consideration to the winds, and impetuously replied :

" I will endeavor to regain this ring for you. Tell me where to go, and whom to attack, and if human wit and strength can compass it, you shall have the jewel back before morning."

" Oh ! " she protested, " I see that you anticipate a task of small difficulty. You cannot recover this particular ring so easily as that. In the first place, I do not in the least know who took it ; I only know its destination.

Alas! if it is allowed to reach that destination, I am bereft of hope."

"No love token," I murmured, "and yet your whole peace depends on its recovery."

"More than my peace," she answered; and with a quick movement she closed the door which I had left open behind me. As its sharp bang rang through the room, I realized into what a pitfall I had stumbled. Only a political intrigue of the most desperate character could account for the words I had heard and the actions to which I had been a witness. But I was in no mood to recoil even from such dangers as these, and so my look showed her as she leaned toward me with the words:

"Listen! I am burdened with a secret. I am in this house, in this city, for a purpose. The secret is not my own and I cannot part with it; neither is my purpose communicable. You therefore will be obliged to deal with the greatest dangers blindfold. One encouragement only I can give you. You will work for good ends. You are pitted against wrong, not right, and if you succumb, it will be in a cause you yourself would call noble. Do I make myself understood, Mr.—Mr.——"

"Abbott," I put in, with a bow.

She took the bow for an affirmative, as indeed I meant she should. "You do not recoil," she murmured, "not even when I say that you must take no third party into your confidence, no matter to what extremity you are brought."

"I would not be the man I think I am, if I recoiled," I said, smiling.

She waved her hand with almost a stern air.

"Swear!" she commanded; "swear that, from the moment you leave this door till you return to it, you will breathe no word concerning me, your errand, or even the oath I am now exacting from you."

"Ah!" thought I to myself, "this *is* serious." But I took the oath under the spell of the most forceful personality I had ever met, and did not regret it—*then*.

"Now let us waste no more time," said she.

" In the large building on —— Street there is an office with the name of Dr. Merriam on the door. See! I have written it on this card, so that there may be no mistake about it. That office is open to patients from ten in the morning until twelve at noon. During these hours any one can enter there; but to awaken no distrust, he should have some ailment. Have you not some slight disorder concerning which you might consult a physician?"

"I doubt it," said I; "but I might manufacture one."

"That would not do with Dr. Merriam. He is a skilful man; he would see through any imposture."

"I have a sick friend," I ruminated. "And by the way, his case is obscure and curious. I could interest any doctor in it in five minutes."

"That is good; consult him in regard to your friend; meantime—while you are waiting for the interview, I mean--take notice of a large box you will find placed on a side-table. Do not seem to fix your attention on it, but never let it be really out of your sight from the moment the door is unlocked at ten till you are forced by the doctor's importunity to leave the room at twelve. If you are alone there for one minute (and you will be allowed to remain there alone if you show no haste to consult the doctor) unlock that box—here is the key—and look carefully inside. No one will interfere and no one will criticize you; there is more than one person who has access to that box."

"But—" I put in.

"You will discover there," she whispered, "a hand of bronze lying on an enamelled cushion. On the fingers of this hand there should be, and doubtless are, rings of forged steel of peculiar workmanship. *If there is one on the middle finger*, my cause is lost, and I can only await the end." Her cheek paled. "*But if there is not*, you may be sure that an attempt will be made by some one to-morrow—I do not know whom—to put one there before the office closes at noon. The ring will be mine—the one stolen from my hand just now

—and it will be your business to prevent the box being opened for this purpose, by any means short of public interference involving arrest and investigation; for this, too, would be fatal. The delay of a day may be of incalculable service to me. It would give me time to think, if not to act. Does the undertaking seem a hopeless one? Am I asking too much of your inexperience?"

"It does not seem a hopeful one," I admitted; "but I am willing to undertake the adventure. What are its dangers? And why, if I see the ring on the finger you speak of, cannot I take it off and bring it back to you?"

"Because," said she, answering the last question first, "the ring becomes a part of the mechanism the moment it is thrust over the last joint. You could not draw it off. As for the dangers I allude to, they are of a hidden character, and part of the secret I mentioned. If, however, you exercise your wit, your courage, and a proper amount of strategy, you may escape. Interference must be *proved* against you. That rule, at least, has been held inviolate."

Aghast at the mysterious perils she thus indicated in the path toward which she was urging me, I for one instant felt an impulse to retreat. But adventure of any kind has its allurements for an unoccupied youth of twenty-one, and when seasoned, as this was, by a romantic, if unreasonable, passion, proved altogether too irresistible for me to give it up. Laughing outright in my endeavor to throw off the surplus of my excitement, I drew myself up and uttered some fiery phrase of courage, which I doubt if she even heard. Then I said some word about the doctor, which she at once caught up.

"The doctor," said she, "may know, and may not know, the mysteries of that box. I would advise you to treat him solely as a doctor. He who uses the key you now hold in your hand cannot be too wary; by which I mean too careful or too silent. Oh, that I dared to go there myself! But my agitation would betray me. Besides, my person is known, or this ring would never have been taken from me."

"I will be your deputy," I assured her. "Have you any further instructions?"

"No," said she; "instructions are useless in an affair of this kind. Your actions must be determined by the exigencies of the moment. Meantime, my every thought will be yours. Good-night, sir; pray God, it may not be good-by."

"One moment," I said, as I arose to go. "Have you any objection to telling me your name?"

"I am Miss Calhoun," she said, with a graceful bow.

This was the beginning of my formidable adventure with the bronze hand.

II.

THE QUAKER-LIKE GIRL, THE PALE GIRL, AND THE MAN WITH A BRISTLING MUSTACHE.

THE building mentioned by my new-found friend was well known to me. It was one of the kind in which every other office is unoccupied the year round. Such tenants as gave it the little air of usefulness it possessed were of the bad-pay kind. They gave little concern to their own affairs and less to those of their neighbors. The public avoided the building, and the tenants did nothing to encourage a change. In a populous city, on the corner made by frequented streets, it stood as much alone and neglected as if it were a ruin. Old or young eyes may have looked through its begrimed windows into the busy thoroughfare beneath, but none in the street ever honored the old place with a glance or thought. No one even wasted contempt upon its smoky walls, and few disturbed the accumulated dust upon the stairs or in the dimly-lighted hallways.

Had a place been sought for wherein the utmost secrecy might be observed, surely this was that place. As I neared the door upon which I read the doctor's name, I found myself treading on tip-toe, so impressed had I become by a sense of caution, if not of dread.

I had made every effort to be on hand at precisely ten o'clock, and felt so sure that I had been the first to arrive that I reached out to the door-knob with every expectation of entering, unseen by any one, and possibly unheard. To my dismay, the first twist I gave it resulted in a rusty shriek that set my teeth on edge, and echoed down the gloomy hall. With my flesh creeping, I opened the door and passed into the doctor's outer room.

It was far from being empty. Seated in chairs ranged along two sides of the room, I saw a dozen or more persons, male and female. All wore the preoccupied air that patients are apt to assume while awaiting their turn to be called by the doctor. One amongst the number made an effort at indifference by drawing out and pushing back a nail in the flooring with the sole of her pretty shoe. It may have been intended for coquetry, and at another time might have bewitched me; now it seemed strangely out of place. The man who was to all appearance counting the flies in the web of an industrious spider was more in keeping with the place, my feelings, and the atmosphere of despondency that the room gave out.

As I had no doubt that the ring I was seeking was in the possession of some one of these persons, I gave each as minute an examination as was possible under the circumstances. Only two amongst them appeared open to suspicion. Of these, one was a young man whose naturally fine features would have prepossessed him in my favor had it not been for the peculiar alertness of his bright blue eye, which flashed incessantly in every direction till each and all of us seemed to partake of his restlessness and anxiety. Why was he not depressed? The other was the girl, or, rather, the young lady to whose pretty foot I have referred. If she was at all conspicuous, it was owing to the contrast between her beautiful face and the Quaker-like simplicity of her dress. She was restless also; her foot had ceased its action, but her hand moved constantly. Now it clutched its fellow in her lap, and now it ran in an oft-repeated action, seemingly beyond her control, up and down and round and round a plain but expensive leather bag she wore at her side. "She carries the ring," thought I, sitting down in the chair next her.

Meantime, I had not been oblivious of *the box*. It stood upon a plain oak table directly opposite the door by which I had come in. It was about a foot square, and was the only object in the room at all ornamental. Indeed, there was but little else for the eye to rest on, consequently most of us looked that way, though I noticed that but few seemed to take any real interest in that or anything else within sight. This was encouraging, and I was on the point of transferring my entire attention to the two persons I have named, when one of them, the nearest, rose hurriedly and went out.

This was an unexpected move on her part, and I did not know what to make of it. Had I annoyed her by my scrutiny, or had she divined my errand? In my doubt, I consulted the face of the man I secretly thought to be her accomplice. It was non-committal, and, in my doubt as to the meaning of all this, I allowed myself to become interested in a pale young woman who had been sitting on the other side of the lady who had just left. She was evidently a patient who stood in great need of assistance. Her head hung feebly forward, and her whole figure looked ready to drop. Yet when a minute later the door of the inner office opened, and the doctor appeared on the sill in an expectant attitude, she made no attempt to rise, but pushed forward another woman who seemed less indisposed than herself. I had to compel myself to think of all I saw as being real and within my experience.

Surprised by this action on the part of one so ill, I watched the pale girl for an instant, and almost forgot my mission in the compassion aroused by her sickly appearance. But soon that mission and my motive for being in this place were somewhat vividly recalled to me by an unexpected action on this very young woman's part. With the sudden movement of an acutely suffering person, she bounded from her seat and crossed the floor to where the box stood, gasping for breath, and almost falling against the table when she reached it.

A grunt from the good-looking young man followed; but neither he nor the middle-aged female with a pitiful skin disease, who had been sitting near her, offered to go to her assistance, though the latter looked as if she would like to. I was the only one to rise. The truth is, I could see no one touch *the box* without having something more than my curiosity awakened. Approaching her respectfully, and with as complete a dissimulation of my real feelings as possible, I ventured to say:

"You are very ill, miss. Shall I summon the doctor?"

She was clutching the side of the table for support, and her head, drooping helplessly over the box, was swaying from side to side as she rocked to and fro in her pain.

"Thank you!" she gasped, without turning, "I will wait. I would rather wait."

At that moment the doctor's door opened again.

"There he is now," said I.

"I will wait," she insisted. "Let the others take their turn."

Satisfied now that something besides pain caused her interest in the box, I drew back, asking myself whether she had been in possession of the ring from the beginning, or whether it had been passed to her by her restless neighbor. Meanwhile, another patient had disappeared into the adjoining room.

A few minutes passed. The man with the

restless eye began to fidget. Could it be that she was simply guarding the box, and that he was the one who wished to open it? As the doubt struck me, I surveyed her more attentively. She was certainly doing something besides supporting herself with that sly right hand of hers. Yes, that was a click I heard. She was fitting a key into the lock. Startled, but determined not to betray myself, I assumed an air of great patience, and, taking a memorandum book from my pocket, began to write in it. Meantime, the doctor had disposed of his second patient and had beckoned to a third. To my astonishment, my friend with the nervous manner responded, thus acquitting himself in my eyes from any interest in the box.

The interview he had with the doctor lasted some time; meantime, the young woman in the window remained more or less motionless. When the fourth person left the room, she turned and cast a quick glance at myself and the other person present.

I knew what it meant. She was anxious to

be left alone in order to lift that mysterious lid. She was no more ill than I was.

There was even a dash of color in her cheeks, and the trembling she indulged in was caused by great excitement and suspense, and not by pain.

Compassion at once gave way to anger, and I inwardly resolved not to spare her if we came into conflict over the box.

My companion was an old and non-observant man, who had come in after the rest of us. When the doctor again appeared, I motioned to this old man to follow him, which he very gladly did, leaving me alone with the pale girl. At once I got up, showing my fatigue and slightly yawning.

" This is very tedious," I muttered aloud, and stepped idly towards the door leading into the hall.

The girl at the box could not restrain her impatience. She cast me another short glance. I affected not to see it ; took out my watch, consulted it, put it back quickly and slipped out into the hall. As I closed the door behind me, I heard a slight creak. Instantly I was back again, and with so sudden a movement that I surprised her, with her face bent over the open box.

"Oh, my poor young lady," I exclaimed, springing towards her with every appearance of great concern. "You do not look able to stand. Lean on me if you feel faint, and I will help you to a seat."

She turned upon me in a fury, but, meeting my eye, assumed an air of composure, which did not impose upon me in the least, or prevent me from pressing close to her side and taking one look into the box, which she had evidently not had sufficient self-possession to close.

The sight which met my eye was not unexpected, yet was no less interesting on that account. A hand—*the* hand—curiously made of bronze, and of exquisite proportions, lay on its enamelled cushion, with rings on all of its fingers save one. That one I was delighted to see was the middle one, proof positive that the mischief contemplated by Miss Calhoun had not yet been accomplished.

Restored to complete self-possession by this discovery, I examined the box and its contents with an air of polite curiosity. I surprised myself by my self-possession and *bonhomie*.

"What an odd thing to find in a physician's office!" I exclaimed. "Beautiful, is it not? An unusual work of art; but there is nothing in it to alarm you. You shouldn't allow yourself to be frightened at such a thing as that." And with a quick action, she was wholly powerless to prevent, I shut down the lid, which closed with a snap.

Startled and greatly discomposed, she drew back, hastily thrusting her hand behind her.

"You are very officious," she began, but, seeing nothing but good nature in the smile with which I regarded her, she faltered irresolutely, and finally took refuge again in her former trick of invalidism. Breaking out into low moanings, she fell back upon the nearest chair, from which she immediatel y started again with the quick cry, "Oh, how I suffer! I am not well enough to be out alone." And turning with a celerity that belied her words, she fled into the hall, shutting the door violently behind her.

Astonished at the completeness of my victory, I spent the first moments of triumph in trying to lift the lid of the box. But it was securely locked. I was just debating whether I could now venture to return to my seat, when the hall door reopened and a gentleman entered.

He was short, sturdy and had a bristling black mustache. I needed to look at him but once to be certain he was interested both in the box and me, and, while I gave no evidence of my discovery, I prepared myself for an adventure of a much more serious nature than that which had just occupied me.

Modeling my behavior upon that of the young girl whose place I had usurped, I placed my elbow on the box and looked out of the window. As I did so I heard a shuffling in the adjoining room, and knew that in another moment the doctor would again appear at the door to announce that he was ready for another patient. How could I evade the summons? The man behind me was a determined one. He was there for the purpose of opening the box, and would not be likely to leave the room while I remained in it. How, then, could I comply with the requirements of the situation and yet prevent this new-comer from lifting the lid in my absence? I knew of but one way—a way which had suggested itself to me during the long watches of the previous night, and which I had come prepared to carry out.

Taking advantage of my proximity to the box, I inserted in the keyhole a small morsel of wax which for some minutes past I had been warming in my hand. This done, I laid my hat down on the lid, noting with great exactness as I did so just where its rim lay in reference to the various squares and scrolls with which the top was ornamented. By this means I felt that I might know if the hat were moved in my absence. The doctor having showed himself by this time, I followed him into his office with a calmness born of the most complete confidence in the strategy I had employed.

Dr. Merriam, whom I have purposely refrained from describing until now, was a tall, well-made man, with a bald head and a pleasant eye, but careless in his attire and bearing. As I met that eye and responded to his good-natured greeting, I inwardly decided that his interest in the box was much less than his guardianship of it would seem to betoken. And when I addressed him and entered upon the subject of my friend's complaint, I soon saw by the depth of his professional interest that whatever connection he might have with the box, neither that nor any other topic whatever could for a moment vie with his delight in a new and strange case like that of my poor friend. I consequently entered into the medical details demanded of me with a free mind and succeeded in getting some very valuable advice, for which I was of course truly grateful.

As soon as this was accomplished I took my leave, but not by the usual door of egress. Saying that I had left my hat in the ante-room, I bowed my acknowledgments to the doctor and returned the way I came. But not without meeting with a surprise. There was still but one person in the room with the box, but that person was not the man with the bristling mustache and determined eye whom I had expected to find there. It was the pretty, Quaker-like girl who had formerly aroused my suspicions; and though she sat far from the box, a moment's glance at her flushed face and trembling hands assured me she had but that moment left it.

Going at once to the box, I saw that my hat had been moved. But more significant still was the hairpin lying on the floor at my feet, with a morsel of wax sticking to one of its points. This was conclusive. The man had discovered why his key would not work, and had called to his aid the young lady, who had evidently been waiting in the hall outside.

She had tried to pick out the wax—a task in which I had happily interrupted her.

Proud of the success of my device, and satisfied that the danger was over for that day (it being well on to twelve o'clock), I said a few words more to the doctor, who had followed me into the room, and then prepared to take my departure. But the young lady was more agile than I. Saying something about a very pressing engagement which would not allow her to consult the doctor that day, she hurried ahead of me and ran quickly down the long hall. The doctor looked astonished, but dismissed the matter with a shrug ; while, with the greatest desire to follow her, I stood hesitating on the threshold, when my eye fell on a small object lying under the chair on which she had been sitting. It was the little leathern bag I had seen hanging at her side.

Catching it up, I explained that I would run after the young lady and restore it ; and glad of an excuse which would enable me to follow her through the streets without risking the suspicion of impropriety, I hastened down the stairs and happily succeeded in reaching the pavement before her skirts whisked round the corner. I was therefore but a few paces behind her, which distance I took good care to preserve.

III.

MADAME.

My motive in following this young girl was not so much to restore her property, as to see where her engagement was taking her. I felt confident that none of the three persons who had shown interest in the box was the prime mover in an affair so important; and it was necessary above all things to find out who the prime mover was. So I followed the girl.

She led me into a doubtful quarter of the town. As the crowd between us diminished and we reached a point where we were the only pedestrians on the block we were then traversing, I grew anxious lest she should turn and see me before arriving at her destination. But she evidently was without suspicion, for she passed without any hesitation up a certain stoop in the middle of this long block and entered an open door on which a brass plate was to be seen, inscribed with this one word in large black letters:

"MADAME."

This was odd; and as I had no inclination to encounter any "madame" without some hint as to her character and business, I looked about me for some one able and willing to give me the necessary information. An upholsterer's shop in an opposite basement seemed to offer me the opportunity I wanted. Crossing the street, I saluted the honest-looking man I met in the doorway, and pointing out madame's house, asked what was done over there.

He answered with a smile.

"Go and see," he said; "the door's open. Oh, they don't charge anything," he made haste to protest, misunderstanding, no doubt, my air of hesitation. "I was in there once myself. They all sit round and she talks; that is, if she feels like it. It is all nonsense, you know, sir; no good in it."

"But is there any harm?" I asked. "Is the place reputable and safe?"

"Oh, safe enough; I never heard of anything going wrong there. Why, ladies go there; real ladies; veiled, of course. I have seen two carriages at a time standing in front of that door. Fools, to be sure, sir; but honest enough, I suppose."

I needed no further encouragement. Recrossing the street, I entered the house which stood so invitingly open, and found myself almost immediately in a large hall, from which I was ushered by a silent negress into a long room with so dim and mysterious an interior that I felt like a man suddenly transported from the bustle of the out-door world into the mystic recesses of some Eastern temple.

The causes of this effect were simple. A dim

light suggesting worship; the faint scent of slowly burning incense; women and men sitting on low benches about the walls. In the center, on a kind of raised dais, backed by a drapery of black velvet, a woman was seated, in the semblance of a Hindoo god, so nearly did her heavy, compactly crouched figure, wound about with Eastern stuffs and glistening with gold, recall the images we are accustomed to associate with the worship of Vishnu. Her face, too, so far as it was visible in the subdued light, had the unresponsiveness of carven wood, and if not exactly hideous of feature, had in it a strange and haunting quality calculated to impress a sensitive mind with a sense of implacable fate. Cruel, hard, passionless, and yet threatening to a degree, must this countenance have seemed to those who willingly subjected themselves to its baneful influence.

I was determined not to be one of these, and yet I had not regarded her for two minutes before I found myself forgetting the real purpose of my visit, and taking a seat with the rest, in anticipation of something for which as yet I had no name, even in my own mind.

How long I sat there motionless I do not know. A spell was on me—a spell from which I suddenly roused with a start. Why or through what means I do not know. Nobody else had moved. Fearing a relapse into this trance-like state, I made a persistent effort to be freed from its dangers. Happily the full signification of my errand there burst upon me. Finding myself really awake, I ventured to peer about, expecting to see the more willing devotees affected as I had been. I encountered a flash from the eyes of the young lady whose bag I held in my hand. She was under no spell. She had not only seen but recognized me.

I held the bag towards her. She gave a furtive glance in the direction of Madame—a glance not free from fear—then clutched the bag. Before releasing my hold upon it I ventured upon a word of explanation. I got no further, for at this moment a voice was heard.

By the effect it had upon the expectant ones, I knew it could have emanated only from the idol-like being who had filled the place with her awesome personality.

At first the voice sounded like a distant call, musically sweet and low ; the kind of note that we can imagine the Indian snake-charmers to use when the cobra raises its winged head in obedience to the pipe's resistless charm. Every ear was strained to hear ; mine with the rest. So much preparation, so much faith must result in something. What was it to be ? The incoherent sounds became more and more distinct, and, finally, took on the articulate form of words. The quiet was deathly. Every one was prepared to interpret her utterances into personal significance. The dread and trouble of the times filling all minds, men wished to be forehanded with the decrees of Providence. Into this brooding silence the low, vibrating tones of this mysterious voice entered, and this is what we heard :

" *Doom ! doom ! For him—the one—the be-*

trayer—the passing bell is tolling. Hear it, ye weak ones and grow strong. Hear it, ye mighty and tremble. Not alone for him will it ring. For ye! for ye! if the decree of the linked rings goes forth——"

Here there was a perceptible quiver of the drapery back of the dais. Others may not have noted it; I did. When, therefore, a very white hand came slowly from between its folds and placed its fingers upon the right temple of Madame, I was not much startled. What did startle me was the fact let out before that admonishing hand touched her, that this being —I can hardly call her woman—seemingly so far removed from the political agitations of the day, was, in very deed, either consciously or unconsciously—I could not decide which—intimately connected with the conspiracy I was at that very moment striving to defeat. How intimately? Was she the prime mover I was seeking, or simply an instrument under the control of another, and yet stronger, personality imaged in the owner of that white hand?

There was no means of determining at that moment. Meanwhile, the fingers had left the temple of Madame. The hand was slowly withdrawn. Sleep apparently fell again upon the dreamer, but only long enough for her to bring forth the words:

"I have said."

The silence that followed, gave me time to think. It was necessary. She had bidden the mighty tremble and had pronounced death to one—the betrayer. Was this senseless drivel, prophetic sight, or threatened murder? I inclined to consider it the last, and this was why: For some weeks now, murder, or, at least, sudden death, had been rampant in the country. My flesh crept as I remembered the many mysterious deaths reported within the month from St. Louis, Boston, New Orleans, New York and even here in Baltimore. Like a flash it came across me that every name was identified, more or less closely, with the political affairs of the time. Coupling my knowledge with what I conjectured, was it strange I saw a confirmation of the worst fears expressed by Miss Calhoun in the half-completed sentences of this seeming clairvoyant?

So occupied had I been with my own thoughts that I feared I might have done something to call an undesirable attention to myself. Glancing furtively to one side, I heard, in the opposite direction, these words:

"She has never failed. What she has said will come to pass. Some one of note will die."

These gloomy words were the first to break the ominous silence. Turning to face the speaker, I encountered the cold eye of a man with a retreating chin, a receding forehead, and a mouth large and cruel enough to stamp him as one of those perverted natures who, to the unscrupulous, are usefully insane.

Here, then, was a being who not only knew the meaning of the fateful words we had heard, but, to my mind, could be relied upon to make them a verity.

It was a relief to me to turn my gaze from his repellant features to the fixed countenance of Madame. She had not stirred ; but either the room had grown lighter or my eyes had become more accustomed to the darkness, for I certainly saw a change in her look. Her eyelids were now raised, and her eyes were bent directly upon me. This was uncomfortable, especially as there was malevolence in her glance, or so I thought, and, far from being pleased with my position, I began to wish that I had never allowed myself to enter the place. Under the influence of this feeling I let my eyes drop from the woman's countenance to her hands, which were folded, as I have said, in a fixed position across her breast. The result was an increase of my mental disturbance. They were brown, shining hands, laden with rings, and, in the added light, under which I saw them, bore a strange resemblance to the bronze hand I had just left in Dr. Merriam's office.

I had never considered myself a weak man, but, from that instant, I began to have a crawling fear of this woman—a fear that was in nowise lessened by the very evident agitation visible in the girl, who had been for me the connecting link between that object of mystery and this.

Unendurable quiet was upon us all again. It was aggravated by awe—an awe to which I was determined not to succumb, notwithstanding the secret uneasiness under which I was laboring. So I let my eyes continue to roam, till they fell upon the one thing moving in the room. This was a man's foot, which I now saw projecting from behind the drapery through which I had seen the white hand glide. It was swinging up and down in an impatient way, so out of keeping with the emotions perceptible on this side of the drapery that I felt forced to ask myself what sort of person this could be who thus kept watch and ward with such very commonplace impatience over a creature who was able to hold every other person in her presence under a spell. The drapery did not give up its secrets, and again I yielded to the fascinations of Madame's face.

There was a change in it ; the eyes no longer looked my way, but into space, which seemed to hold for them some terrible and heart-rending vision. The lips, which had been closed, were now parted, and from them issued a breath which soon formed itself into words.

"'Vengeance is mine! I will repay,' saith the Lord." What passionate utterance was this? The voice that had been musical now rang with jangling discord. The swinging of the foot behind the drapery ceased. Madame spoke on:

"Through pain, sorrow, blood and death shall victory come. Life for life, pang for pang, scorn for scorn!"

The swinging foot disappeared, and the small white hand passed quickly through the curtain and rested again upon the forehead of Madame. But without a calming effect this time. On the contrary, it seemed to urge and incite her, for she broke into a new strain, speaking rapidly, wildly, as if she lived in what she saw, or, what was doubtless truer, had lived in it and was but recalling her own past in one of those terrible hours of memory that recur on the border-land of dreams.

"I see a child, a girl. She is young; she is beautiful. Men love her, many men, but she loves only one. He is of the North; she is of the South. He is icy like his clime; she is fiery like her skies. The fire cannot warm the ice. It is the ice puts out the fire! Woe! woe!"

The left hand came from the drapery; found its way to the left temple of the woman. But it, too, was ineffectual. Hurriedly, madly, the words went on, tripping each other up in their haste and passion. The voice now became hoarse with rage.

"The girl is now a woman. A child is given her. The man demands the child. She will not give it up. He curses it; he curses her, but she is firm and holds it to her breast till her arms are blackened by the blows he deals her. Then he curses her *country*, the land that gave her a *heart;* and, hearing this, she rises up and curses him and his with an oath the Lord will hear and answer from His judgment throne. *For the child was slain between them* and its pitiful, small body blocks the passage of Mercy between his and hers forever. Woe! woe!"

As suddenly as the vehement change had come upon her, she had become calm again. The eyes retained their stony stare, but a cold and cruel smile formed about her lips, as if, with the utterance of that last word, she saw a futurity of blood and carnage satisfying her ferocious soul.

It was revolting, horrible; but no one else seemed to feel it as I did. To most it was a short glimpse into a suffering soul. To me it was the revelation of causes which had led, and would lead yet, to miseries for which she had no pity, and which I felt myself too weak to avert.

That it was not intended that the devotees of Madame should have heard these ravings was evident; for at this juncture the owner of the two white hands that had failed to control the spirit of Madame came out from behind the drapery of the dais. He proved to be none other than the man with the bristling mustache whose plans I had disarranged at the doctor's office by plugging the keyhole of the box with wax.

This was enough. "Chicanery!" was my inmost thought as I noted his cool and calculating eye. "But very dangerous chicanery," I added. Was the ring upon whose immediate capture I now saw that a life, if not lives, depended, in his possession, or in that of Madame, or in that of the Quaker-like girl sitting a few seats from me? How impossible to tell, and yet how imperative to know! As I was debating how this could be brought about, I watched the man.

Self-control was a habit with him, but I saw the nervous clutch of his delicate hand. This did not indicate complete mastery of himself at that moment. He spoke with care, but as if he were in haste to deliver himself of the few necessary words of dismissal, without betraying his lack of composure.

"Madame will awake presently; she will be heard no more to-day. Those who wish to kiss her robes may pass in front of her; but she is still too far away from earth to hear your voices or to answer any questions. You will therefore preserve silence."

So! so! more chicanery. Or was it strategy, pure and simple? Was there at the bottom of his words the wish to see me nearer or was he just playing with the credulity of such believers as the man next me, for instance? I did not stop to determine. My anxiety to see Madame, without the illusion of even the short distance between us, induced me to join the file of the faithful who were slowly approaching the seated woman. I would not kiss her robes, but I would look into her eyes and make sure that she was as far away from us all as she was said to be.

But as I drew nearer to her I forgot all about her eyes in the interest awakened by her hands. And when it came my turn to pause before her, it was upon the middle finger of her right hand my eyes were fixed. For there I saw THE RING; the veritable ring of my fair neighbor, if the description given by her was correct.

To see it there was to have it; or so I vowed in my surprise and self-confidence. Putting on an air of great dignity, I bowed to the woman and passed on, resolving upon the course I would pursue, which must necessarily be daring in order to succeed. At the door I paused till all who followed me had passed out; then I turned back, and once again faced Madame.

She was alone. Her watchful guardian had left her side, and to all appearances the room. The opportunity surpassed my expectations, and with a step full of nerve I pushed forward and took my stand again directly in front of her. She gave no token of seeing me; but I did not hesitate on that account. Exerting all my will power, I first subjected her to a long and masterful look, and then I spoke, directly and to the point, like one who felt himself her superior.

"Madame," said I, "the man you wish for is here. Give me the ring, and trust no more to weak or false emissaries."

The start with which she came to life, or to the evidence of life, was surprising. Lifting her great lids, she returned my gaze with one equally searching and powerful, and seeing with what disdain I sustained it, allowed an almost imperceptible tremor to pass across her face, which up to now had not displayed the shadow even of an emotion.

"You!" she murmured, in a dove-like tone of voice; "who are you that I should trust you more than the others?"

"I am he you expect," said I, venturing more as I felt her impassibility giving way before me. "Have you had no premonition of my coming? Did you not know that he who controls would be in your presence to-day?"

She trembled, and her fingers almost unclasped from her arms.

"I have had dreams," she murmured, "but I have been bidden to beware of dreams. If you are the person you claim to be, you will have some token which will absolve me from the charge of credulity. What is your token?"

Though doubtful, I dared not hesitate. "This," I said, taking from my pocket the key which had been given me by my fair neighbor.

She moved, she touched it with a finger; then she eyed me again.

"Others have keys," said she, "but they fail in the opening. How are you better than they?"

"You know," I declared—"you know that I can do what others have failed in. Give me the ring."

The force, the assurance with which I uttered this command moved her in spite of herself. She trembled, gave me one final, searching look, and slowly began to pull the ring from off her finger. It was in her hand, and half way to mine, when a third voice came to break the spell.

"Madame, Madame," it said; "be careful. This is the man who clogged the lock, and hindered my endeavors in your behalf in the doctor's office."

Her hand which was so near mine drew back; but I was too quick and too determined for her. I snatched the ring before she could replace it on her own hand, and, holding it firmly, faced the intruder with an air of very well-assumed disdain.

"Attempt no argument with me. It was because I saw your weakness and vulgar self-confidence that I interfered in a matter only to be undertaken by one upon whom all can rely. Now that I have the ring, the end is near. Madame, be wiser in the choice of your confidants. *To-morrow this ring will be in its proper place.*"

Bowing as I had done before, I advanced to the door. They had made no effort to regain the ring, and I felt that my rashness had stood me in good stead. But as, with a secret elation I was just capable of keeping within bounds, I put my foot across the threshold, I heard behind me a laugh so triumphant and mocking that I felt struck with consternation; and, glancing down into my hand, I saw that I held, not the peculiar steel circlet destined for the piece of mechanism in the doctor's office, but an ordinary ring of gold.

She had offered me the wrong ring, *and I had taken it*, thus proving the falsity of my pretensions.

There was nothing left for me but to acknowledge defeat by an ignominious departure.

IV.

CHECKMATE.

I HASTENED at once home, and knocked at Miss Calhoun's door. While waiting for a response, the mockery of my return without the token I had undertaken to restore to her, impressed itself upon me in full force. It seemed to me that in that instant my face must have taken on a haggard look. I could not summon up the necessary will to make it otherwise. Any effort in that direction would have made my failure at cheerfulness pitiable.

The door opened. There she stood. Whatever expectancy of success she may have had fled at once. Our eyes met and her countenance changed. My face must have told the whole story, for she exclaimed :

"You have failed ! "

I was obliged to acknowledge it in a whisper, but hastened to assure her that the ring had not yet been placed upon the bronze hand, and was not likely to be till the lock had been cleaned out. This interested her, and called out a hurried but complete recital of my adventure. She hung upon it breathlessly, and when I reached the point where Madame and her prophetic voice entered the tale, she showed so much excitement that any doubts I may have cherished as to the importance of the communication Madame had made us vanished in a cold horror I with difficulty hid from my companion. But the end agitated her more than the beginning, and when she heard that I had taken upon myself a direct connection with this mysterious matter, she grew so pale that I felt forced to inquire if the folly I had committed was likely to result badly, at which she shuddered and replied:

"You have brought death upon yourself. I see nothing but destruction before us both. This woman—this horrible woman—has seen your face, and, if she is what you describe, she will never forget it. The man, who is her guardian or agent, no doubt, must have tracked you, and finding you here with me, from whose hand he himself may have torn the ring last night, will record it as treason against a cause which punishes all treason with death.

"Pshaw!" I ejaculated, with a jocular effort at indifference, which I acknowledge I did not feel. "You seem to forget the law. We live in the city of Baltimore. Charlatans such as I have just left behind me do not make away with good citizens with impunity. We have only to seek the protection of the police."

She met my looks with a slowly increasing

intentness, which stilled this protest on my lips.

"I am under no oath," she ruminated. "I can tell this man what I will. Mr. Abbott, there has been formed in this city an organization against which the police are powerless. I am an involuntary member of it, and I know its power. It has constrained me and it has constrained others, and no one who has opposed it once has lived to do so twice. Yet it has no recognized head (though there is a chief to whom we may address ourselves), and it has no oaths of secrecy. All is left to the discretion of its members, and *to their fears*. The object of this society is the breaking of the power of the North, and the means by which it works is *death*. I joined it under a stress of feeling I called patriotism, and I believed myself right till the sword was directed against my own breast. Then I quailed; then I began to ask by what right we poor mortals constitute ourselves into instruments of destruction to our kind, and having once stopped to question, I saw the whole matter in such a different light that I knowingly put a stumbling-block in the path of so-called avenging justice, and thus courted the doom that at any moment may fall upon my head." And she actually looked up, as if expecting to see it fall then and there. "This Madame," she went on in breathless haste, 'is doubtless one of the members. How so grotesque and yet redoubtable an individuality should have become identified with a cause demanding the coolest judgment as well as the most acute political acumen, I cannot stop to conjecture. But that she is a member of our organization, and an important one, too, her prophecies, which have so strangely become facts, are sufficient proof, even had you not seen my ring on her finger. Perhaps, incredible as it may appear, she is the *chief*. If so— But I do not make myself intelligible," she continued, meeting my eyes. "I will be more explicit. One peculiar feature of this organization is the complete ignorance which we all have concerning our fellow-members. We can reveal nothing, for we know nothing. I know that I am allied to a cause which has for its end the destruction of all who oppose the supremacy of the South, but I cannot give you the name of another person attached to this organization, though I feel the pressure of their combined power upon every act of my life. *You* may be a member without my knowing it—a secret and fearful thought, which forms one of the greatest safeguards to the institution, though it has failed in this instance, owing'—'here her voice fell—" to my devotion to the man I love. What?"—(I had not spoken; my heart was dying within me, but I had given no evidence of a wish to interrupt her; she, however, feared a check, and rushed vehemently on.) " I shall have to tell you more. When, through pamphlets and unsigned letters—dangerous communications, which have long since become ashes—I was drawn into this society (and only those of the most radical and impressionable natures are approached) a ring and a key were sent me with this injunction: 'When the man or woman whose name will be forwarded to you in an otherwise empty envelope, shall have, in your honest judgment, proved himself or herself sufficiently dangerous to the cause we love, to merit removal, you are to place this ring on the middle finger of the bronze hand locked up in the box openly displayed in the office of a Dr. Merriam on —— Street. With the pressure of the whole five rings on the fingers of this piece of mechanism, the guardian of our rights will be notified by a bell, that a victim awaits justice, and the end to be accomplished will be begun. As there are five fingers, and each one of these must feel the pressure of its own ring before connection can be made between this hand and the bell mentioned, no injustice can be done and no really innocent person destroyed. For, when five totally disconnected persons devoted to the cause agree that a certain individual is worthy of death, mistake is impossible. You are now one of the five. Use the key and the ring according to your conscience.' This was well, if I had been allowed to follow my conscience; but when, six weeks ago, they sent me the name of a man of lofty character and unquestioned loyalty, I recoiled, scarcely believing my eyes. Yet, fearing that my own judgment was warped, or that some hidden hypocrisy was latent in a man thus given over to our attention, I made it my business to learn this man's inner life. I found it so beautiful——" She choked, turned away for a moment, controlled herself, and went on rapidly and with increased earnestness: "I learned to love this man, and as I learned to love him I grew more and more satisfied of the dangerous character of the organization I was pledged to. But I had one comfort. He could not be doomed without my ring, and that was safe on my finger. Safe! You know how safe it was. The monster whom you have just seen, and who may have been the person to subject this noble man to suspicion, must have discovered my love and the safeguard it offered to this man. The ring, as you know, was stolen, and as you have failed to recover it, and I to get any reply from the chief to whom I forwarded my protest, to-morrow will without doubt see it placed upon the finger of the bronze hand. The result you know. Fantastic as this may strike you, it is the dreadful truth."

Love, had I ever felt this holy passion for her, had no longer a place in my breast; but awe, terror and commiseration for her, for him, and also perhaps for myself, were still active passions within me, and at this decided statement of the case, I laughed in the excitement of the moment, and the relief I felt at knowing just what there was to dread in the adventure.

"Absurd!" I cried. "With Madame's address in my mind and the Baltimore police at my command, this man is as safe from assault as you or I are. Give me five minutes' talk with Chief——"

Her hand on my arm stopped me; the look in her eye made me dumb.

"What could you do without *me?*" she said; "and my evidence you cannot have. For what would give it weight can never pass my lips. The lives that have fallen with my connivance stand between me and confession. I do not wish to subject myself to the law."

This placed her in another light before me, and I started back.

"You have——" I stammered.

"Placed that ring three times on the hand in Dr. Merriam's office."

"And each time?"

"A man somewhere in this nation has died suddenly. I do not know by what means or by whose hand, but he died."

This beautiful creature guilty of —— I tried not to show my horror.

"It is, then, a question of choice between you and him?" said I. "Either you or he must perish. Both cannot be saved."

She recoiled, turning very pale, and for several minutes stood surveying me with a fixed gaze as if overcome by an idea which threw so immense a responsibility upon her. As she stood thus, I seemed not only to look into her nature, but her life. I saw the fanaticism that that had once held every good impulse in check, the mistaken devotion, the unreasoning hatred, and, underneath all, a spirit of truth and rectitude which brightened and brightened as I watched her, till it dominated every evil passion and made her next words come easily, and with a natural burst of conviction which showed the innate generosity of her soul.

"You have shown me my duty, sir. There can be no question as to where the choice should fall. I am not worth one hair of his noble head. Save him, sir; I will help you by every means in my power."

Seizing the opportunity she thus gave me, I asked her the name of the man who was threatened.

In a low voice she told me.

I was astonished; dumfounded.

"Shameful!" I cried. "What motive, what reason can they have for denouncing *him?*"

"He is under suspicion—that is enough."

"Great heaven!" I exclaimed. "Have we reached such a pass as that?"

"Don't," she uttered, hoarsely; "don't reason; don't talk; act."

"I will," I cried, and rushed from the room. She fell back in a chair, almost fainting. I saw her lying quiet, inert and helpless as I rushed by her door on my way to the street, but I did not stop to aid her. I knew she would not suffer it.

The police are practical, and my tale was an odd one. I found it hard, therefore, to impress them with its importance, especially as in trying to save Miss Calhoun I was necessarily more or less incoherent. I did succeed, however, in awakening interest at last, and, a man being assigned me, I led the way to Madame's door. But here a surprise awaited me. The doorplate, which had so attracted my attention, was gone, and in a few minutes we found that she had departed also, leaving no trace behind her.

This looked ominous, and with little delay we hastened to the office of Dr. Merriam. Knocking at the usual door brought no response, but when we tried the further one, by which his patients usually passed out, we found ourselves confronted by the gentleman we sought.

His face was calm and smiling, and though he made haste to tell us that we had come out of hours, he politely asked us in and inquired what he could do for us.

Not understanding how he could have forgotten me so soon, I looked at him inquiringly, at which his face lighted up, and he apologetically said:

" I remember you now. You were here this morning consulting me about a friend who is afflicted with a peculiar complaint. Have you anything further to state or ask in regard to it. I have just five minutes to spare."

" Hear this gentleman first," said I, pointing to the officer who accompanied me,

The doctor calmly bowed, and waited with the greatest self-possession for him to state his case.

The officer did so abruptly.

"There is a box in your ante-room which I feel it my duty to examine. I am Detective Hopkins, of the city police."

The doctor, with a gentleness which seemed native rather than assumed, quietly replied:

"I am very sorry, but you are an hour too late." And, throwing open the door of communication between the two rooms, he pointed to the table.

The box was gone!

V.

DOCTOR MERRIAM.

THIS second disappointment was more than I could endure. Turning upon the doctor with undisguised passion, I hotly asked:

"Who has taken it? Describe the person

at once. Tell what you know about the box, or——"

I did not finish the threat; but my looks must have been very fierce, for he edged off a bit, and cast a curious glance at the officer before he answered:

"You have, then, no ailing friend? Well, well; I expended some very good advice upon you. But you paid me, and so we are even."

"The box!" I urged; "the box! Don't waste words, for a man's life is at stake."

His surprise was marvelously assumed or very real.

"You are talking somewhat wildly, are you not?" he ventured, with a bland air. "A man's life? I cannot believe that."

"But you don't answer me," I urged.

He smiled; he evidently thought me out of my mind.

"That's true; but there is so little I can tell you. I do not know what was in the box about which you express so much concern, and I do not know the names of its owners. It was brought here some six months ago and placed in the spot where you saw it this morning, upon conditions that were satisfactory to me, and not at all troublesome to my patients, whose convenience I was bound to consult. It has remained there till to-day, when——"

Here the officer interrupted him.

"What were these conditions? The matter calls for frankness."

"The conditions," repeated the doctor, in no wise abashed, "were these: That it should occupy the large table in the window as long as they saw fit. That, though placed in my room, it should be regarded as the property of the society which owned it, and, consequently, free to the inspection of its members but to no one else. That I should know these members by their ability to open the box, and that so long as these persons confined their visits to my usual hours for patients, they were to be subject to no one's curiosity, nor allowed to suffer from any one's interference. In return for these slight concessions, I was to receive five dollars for every day I allowed it to stay here, payment to be made by mail."

"Good business! And you cannot tell the names of the persons with whom you entered into this contract?"

"No; the one who came to me first and saw to the placing of the box and all that, was a short, sturdy fellow, with a common face but very brilliant eye; he it was who made the conditions; but the man who came to get it, and who paid me twenty dollars for opening my office door at an unusual hour, was a more gentlemanly man, with a thick, brown mustache and resolute look. He was accompanied——"

"Why do you stop?"

The doctor smiled.

"I was wondering," said he, "if I should say he was accompanied, or that he accompanied, a woman, of such enormous size that the doorway hardly received her. I thought she was a patient at first, for, large as she is, she was brought into my room in a chair, which it took four men to carry. But she only came about the box."

"Madame!" I muttered; and being made still more eager by this discovery of her direct participation in its carrying off, I asked if she touched the box or whether it was taken away unopened.

The doctor's answer put an end to every remaining hope I may have cherished.

"She not only touched but opened it. I saw the lid rise and heard a whirr. What is the matter, sir?"

"Nothing," I made haste to say—"that is, nothing I can communicate just now. This woman must be followed," I signified to the officer, and was about to rush from the room when my eye fell on the table where the box stood.

"See!" said I, pointing to a fine wire protruding from a small hole in the center of its upper surface; "this box had connection with some point outside of this room."

The doctor's face flushed, and for the first time he looked a trifle foolish.

"So I perceive *now*," said he. "The workman who put up this box evidently took liberties in my absence. For *that* I was not paid."

"This wire leads where?" asked the officer.

"Rip up the floor and see. I know no other way to find out."

"But that would take time, and we have not a minute to lose," said I, and was disappearing for the second time when I again stopped. "Doctor," said I, "when you consented to harbor this box under such peculiar conditions and allowed yourself to receive such good pay for a service involving so little inconvenience to yourself, you must have had some idea of the uses to which so mysterious an article would be put. What did you suppose them to be?"

"To tell you the truth, I thought it was some new-fangled lottery scheme, and I have still to learn that I was mistaken."

I gave him a look, but did not stop to undeceive him.

VI.

THE BOX AGAIN.

BUT one resource was left: to warn Mr. S—— of his peril. This was not so easy a task as might appear. To make my story believed, I should be obliged to compromise Miss Calhoun, and Mr. S——'s well-known chivalry, as far as women are concerned, would make the communication difficult on my part, if not absolutely impossible. I, however, determined to attempt it, though I could not but wish I were an older man, with public repute to back me.

Though there was but little in Mr. S——'s public life which I did not know, I had little or no knowledge of his domestic relations beyond the fact that he was a widower with one child. I did not even know where he lived. But inquiry at police headquarters soon settled that, and in half an hour after leaving the doctor's office I was at his home.

It was a large, old-fashioned dwelling, of comfortable aspect; too comfortable, I thought, for the shadow of doom, which, in my eyes, overlay its cheerful front, wide-open doors and windows. How should I tell my story here! What credence could I expect for a tale so gruesome, within walls warmed by so much sunshine and joy. None, possibly; but my story must be told for all that.

Ringing the bell hurriedly, I asked for Mr. S——. He was out of town. This was my first check. When would he be home? The answer gave me some hope, though it seemed to increase my difficulties. He would be in the city by eight, as he had invited a large number of guests to his house for the evening. Beyond this, I could learn nothing.

Returning immediately to Miss Calhoun, I told her what had occurred, and tried to impress upon her the necessity I felt of seeing Mr. S—— that night. She surveyed me like a woman in a dream. Twice did I have to repeat my words before she seemed to take them in; then she turned hurriedly, and going to a little desk standing in one corner of the room, drew out a missive, which she brought me. It was an invitation to this very reception which she had received a week before.

"I will get you one," she whispered. "But don't speak to him, don't tell him without giving me some warning. I will not be far from you. I think I will have strength for this final hour."

"God grant that your sacrifice may bear fruit," I said, and left her.

To enter, on such an errand as mine, a brilliantly illuminated house odoriferous with flowers and palpitating with life and music, would be hard for any man. It was hard for me. But in the excitement of the occasion, aggravated as it was by a presage of danger not only to myself but to the woman I had come so near loving, I experienced a calmness, such as is felt in the presence of all mortal conflicts. I made sure that this was reflected in my face before leaving the dressing-room, and satisfied that I would not draw the attention of others by too much or too little color, I descended to the drawing-room and into the presence of my admired host.

I had expected to confront a handsome man, but not of the exact type that he presented. There was a melancholy in his expression I had not foreseen, mingled with an attraction from which I could not escape after my first hurried glimpse of his features across the wide room. No other man in the room had it to so great a degree, nor was there any other who made so determined an effort to throw off care and be simply the agreeable companion. Could it be that any other warning had forestalled mine, or was this his habitual manner and expression? Finding no answer to this question, I limited myself to the duty of the hour, and advancing as rapidly as possible through the ever-increasing throng, waited for the chance to speak to him for one minute alone. Meantime, I satisfied myself that the two detectives sent from police headquarters were on hand. I recognized them among a group of people at the door.

Whether intentionally or not, Mr. S—— had taken up his stand before the conservatory, and as in my endeavors to reach him I approached within sight of this place, I perceived the face of Miss Calhoun shining from amid its greenery, and at once remembered the promise I had made her. She was looking for me, and, meeting my eyes, made me an imperceptible gesture, to which I felt bound to respond.

Slipping from the group with which I was advancing, I stole around to a side door towards which she had pointed, and in another moment found myself at her side. She was clothed in velvet, which gave to her cheek and brow the colorlessness of marble.

"He is not as ignorant of his position as we thought," said she. "I have been watching him for an hour. He is in anticipation of something. This will make our task easier."

"You have said nothing," I suggested.

"No, no; how could I?"

"Perhaps the detectives I saw there have told him."

"Perhaps; but they cannot know the whole."

"No, or our words would be unnecessary."

"Mr. Abbott," said she, with feverish volubility, "do not try to tell him yet; wait for a few minutes till I have gained a little self-possession, a little command over myself; but no—that may be to risk his life—do not wait a moment—go now, go now, only——" She started, stumbled and fell back into a low seat under a spreading palm. "He is coming here. Do not leave me, Mr. Abbott; step back there behind those plants. I cannot trust myself to face him all alone."

I did as she bade me. Mr. S——, with a smile on his face—the first I had seen there—came in and walked with a quick step and a resolved air up to Miss Calhoun, who endeavored to rise to meet him. But she was unable, which involuntary sign of confusion seemed to please him.

"Irene," said he, in a tone that made me start and wish I had not been so amenable to her wishes, "I thought I saw you glide in here, and my guests being now all arrived, I have ventured to steal away for a moment, just to satisfy the craving which has been torturing me for the last hour. Irene, you are pale; you tremble like an aspen. Have I frightened you by my words—too abrupt, perhaps, considering the reserve that has always been between us until now. Didn't you know that I loved you? that for the last month—ever since I have known you, indeed—I have had but the one wish, to make you my wife?"

"Good God!" I saw the words on her lips rather than heard them. She seemed to be illumined and overwhelmed at once. "Mr. S——," said she, trying to be brave, trying to address him with some sort of self-possession,

"I did not expect—I had no right to expect this honor from you. I am not worthy—I have no right to hear such words from your lips. Besides——" She could go no further; perhaps he did not let her.

"Not worthy—you!" There was infinite sadness in his tone. "What do you think I am, then? It is because you are so worthy, so much better than I am or can ever be, that I want you for my wife. I long for the companionship of a pure mind, a pure hand——"

"Mr. S——" (she had risen, and the resolve in her face made her beauty shine out transcendently), "I have not the pure mind, the pure hand you ascribe to me. I have meddled with matters few women could even conceive of. I am a member—a repentant member, to be sure—of an organization which slights the decrees of God and places the aims of a few selfish souls above the rights of man, and——"

He had stooped and was kissing her hand.

"You need not go on," he whispered; "I quite understand. But you will be my wife?"

Aghast, white as the driven snow, she watched him with dilating eyes that slowly filled with a great horror.

"Understand!—*you understand!* Oh, what does that mean? *Why* should you understand?"

"Because"—his voice sunk to a whisper, but I heard it, as I would have recognized his thought had he not spoken at that moment—"because I am the chief of the organization you mention. Irene, now you have *my* secret."

I do not think she uttered a sound, but I heard the dying cry of her soul in her very silence. He may have heard it, too, for his look showed sudden and unfathomable pity.

"This is a blow to you," he said. "I do not wonder; there *is* something hateful in the fact; latterly I have begun to realize it. That is why I have allowed myself to love. I wanted some relief from my thoughts. Alas! I did not know that a full knowledge of your noble soul would only emphasize them. But this is no talk for a ballroom. Cheer up, darling, and——"

"Wait!" She had found strength to lay her hand on his arm. "Did you know that a man was condemned to-day?"

His face took on a shade of gloom.

"Yes," he bowed, casting an anxious look towards the room from which came the mingled sounds of dance and merriment. "The bell which announces the fact rang during my absence. I did not know there was a name before the society."

She crouched, covering her face with her hands. I think she was afraid her emotion would escape her in a cry. But in an instant they had dropped again, and she was panting in his ear:

"You are the chief and are not acquainted with these matters of life and death? Traitors are these men and women to you—traitors! jealous of your influence and your power!"

He looked amazed; he measured the distance between himself and the door and turned to ask her what she meant, but she did not give him the opportunity.

"Do you know," she asked, "the name of the person for whom the bell rang to-day?"

He shook his head. "I am expecting a messenger with it any moment," said he, looking towards the rear of the conservatory. "Is it any one who is here to-night?"

The gasp she gave might have been heard in the other room. Language and motion seemed both to fail her, and I thought I should have to go to her rescue. But before I could move, I heard the click of a latch at the rear of the conservatory, and saw, peering through the flowers and plants, the wicked face of the man with the receding forehead whom I had seen at madame's, and in his arms he held THE BOX.

It was a shock which sent me further into concealment. Mr. S——, on the contrary, looked relieved. Exclaiming, "Ah, he has come!" he went to the door leading into the drawing-room, locked it, took out the key and returned to meet the stealthy, advancing figure.

The latter presented a picture of malignant joy, horrible to contemplate. The lips of his large mouth were compressed and bloodless. He came on with the quiet certainty and deadly ease of a slimy thing sure of its prey.

As I noted him I felt that not only Mr. S——'s life but my own was not worth a moment's purchase. But I uttered no cry and scarcely breathed. Miss Calhoun, on the contrary, gave vent to a long, shivering sigh. The man bowed as he heard it, but with looks directed solely to Mr. S——.

"I was told," said he, "to deliver this box to you wherever and with whomsoever I should find you. In it you will find *the name*."

Mr. S—— gazed in haughty astonishment, first at the box and then at the man.

"This is irregular," said he. "Why was I not made acquainted with the fact that a name was up for consideration, and why have you removed the box from its place and broken the connection which was made with so much difficulty?"

As he said this he looked up through the glass of the conservatory to a high building I could see towering at the end of the garden. It was the building in which I had first seen that box, and I now understood how this connection had been made.

Mr. S——'s movement had been involuntary. Dropping his eyes, he finished by saying, with an almost imperceptible bow, "You may speak before this lady; she is the holder of a key."

"The connection was broken because suspicion was aroused; to your other question you will find an answer in the box. Shall I open it for you?"

Mr. S——, with a stern frown, shook his head, and produced a key from his pocket. "Do you understand all this?" he suddenly asked Miss Calhoun.

For reply, she pointed to the box.

"Open!" her beseeching looks seemed to say.

Mr. S—— turned the key and threw up the lid. "Look under the hand," suggested the man.

Mr. S—— leaned over the box, which had been laid on a small table, discovered a paper somewhere in its depth, and drew it out. It was no whiter than his face when he did so.

"How many have subscribed to this?" he asked.

"You will observe that there are five rings on the hand," responded the man.

Miss Calhoun started, opened her lips, but paused as she saw Mr. S—— unfold the paper.

"The name of the latest traitor," murmured the man, with a look of ferocity the like of which I had never seen on any human face before.

It was not observed by either of the actors in the tragedy before me. Mr. S—— was gazing with a wild incredulity at the note he had unfolded; she was gazing at him. From the room beyond rose and swelled the sweet strains of the waltz.

Suddenly a low, crackling sound was heard. It came from the paper which Mr. S—— had crumpled in his hand.

"So the society has decreed my death," he said, meeting the man's steel-cold eye for the first time. "Now I know how the men whose doom preceded mine have felt in a presence that leaves no hope to mortal man. But *you* shall not be *my* executioner. I will meet my fate at less noxious hands than yours." And, leaning forward, he whispered a few seemingly significant words into the messenger's ear. The man, grievously disappointed, hung his head, and with a sidelong look, the venom of which made us all shudder, he hesitated to go.

"To-night?" he said.

"To-night," Mr. S—— repeated, and pointed towards the door by which he had entered. Then, as the man still hesitated, he took him by the arm and resolutely led him through the conservatory, crying in his ear, "Go. I am still the chief."

The man bowed, and slipped slowly out into the night.

A burst of music, laughter, voices, joy, rose in the drawing-room. Mr. S—— and Irene Calhoun stood looking at each other.

"You must go home," were the first words he uttered. Then, in a half-reproachful, half-pitiful tone, as if on the verge of tears, he added: "Was I so bad a chief that even you thought me a hindrance to the advancement of the society and the cause to which we are pledged?"

It was the one thing he could say capable of rousing her.

"Oh!" she cried, "it is all a mistake, all a cheat. Did you not get the letter I sent to my chief this morning, written in the usual style and directed in the usual way?"

"No," he answered.

"Then there is worse treason than yours among the five. I wrote to say that my ring had been stolen; that I did not subscribe to the condemnation of the man under suspicion, and that, if it was made, it would be through fraud. That was before I knew that the suspected one and the man I addressed were one and the same. Now——"

"Well, now?"

"You have but to accuse the woman called Madame. The man you have just sent away would forgive you his disappointment if you gave him the supreme satisfaction of carrying doom to the still more formidable being who prophesies death to those for whom she has already prepared a violent end."

"Irene!"

But her passion had found vent and she was not to be stilled. Telling him the whole story of the last twenty-four hours, she waited for the look of comfort she evidently expected. But it did not come. His first words showed why.

"Madame is inexorable," said he; "but Madame is but one of five. There are three others—true men, sound men, thinking men. If they deem me unworthy—and I have shown signs of faltering of late—Madame's animosity or your loving weakness must not stand in the way of their decree. It shall never be said I sanctioned the doom of other men and shrank from my own. I would be unworthy of your love if I did, and your love is everything to me now." She had not expected this; she had not at all reckoned upon the stern quality in this man, forgetting that without it he could never have held his pitiless position.

"But it is not regular; it is not according to precedent. Five rings are required, and only four were fairly placed. As an honest man, you ought to hesitate at injustice, and injustice you will show if you allow them to triumph through their own deceit."

But even this failed to move him.

"I see five rings," said he, "and I see another thing. Never will I be permitted to live even if I am coward enough to take advantage of the loophole of escape you offer me. A man who is once seen to tremble loses the confidence of such men as call me *chief*. I would die suddenly, horribly and perhaps when less prepared for it than now. And you, my darling, my imperial one! you would not escape. Besides, you have forgotten the young man who, with such unselfishness, has lent himself to your schemes in my favor. What could save him if I disappointed the malignancy of Madame. No; I have destroyed others, and must submit to the penalty incurred by murder. Kiss me, Irene, and go. I command it as your chief."

With a low moan she gave up the struggle. Lifting her forehead to his embrace, she bestowed upon him a look of indescribable despair, then tottered to the door leading into the garden. As it closed upon her departing figure, he uttered a deep sigh, in which he seemed to give up life and the world. Then he raised his head, and in an instant was in the midst of a throng of beautiful women and dashing men, with a smile on his lips and a jest on his tongue.

I made my escape unnoticed. The next morning I was in Philadelphia. There I read the following lines in the leading daily:

"BALTIMORE, MD.—An unexpected tragedy occurred here last evening. Mr. S——, the well-known financier and politician, died at his supper-table, while drinking the health of a hundred assembled guests. He is considered to be a great loss to the Southern cause. The city is filled with mourning."

And further down, in an obscure corner, this short line:

"BALTIMORE, MD.—A beautiful young woman, known by the name of Irene Calhoun, was found dead in her bed this morning, from the effects of poison administered by herself. No cause is ascribed for the act."

MIDNIGHT IN BEAUCHAMP ROW

MIDNIGHT IN BEAUCHAMP ROW.[1]

IT was the last house in Beauchamp Row, and it stood several rods away from its nearest neighbor. It was a pretty house in the daytime, but owing to its deep, sloping roof and small bediamonded windows it had a lonesome look at night, notwithstanding the crimson hall-light which shone through the leaves of its vine-covered doorway.

Ned Chivers lived in it with his six months' married bride, and as he was both a busy fellow and a gay one there were many evenings when pretty Letty Chivers sat alone until near midnight.

She was of an uncomplaining spirit, however, and said little, though there were times when both the day and evening seemed very long and married life not altogether the paradise she had expected.

On this evening—a memorable evening for her, the twenty-fourth of December, 1894—she had expected her husband to remain with her, for it was not only Christmas eve, but the night when, as manager of a large manufacturing concern, he brought up from New York the money with which to pay off the men on the next working day, and he never left her when there was any unusual amount of money in the house. But from the first glimpse she had of him coming up the road she knew she was to be disappointed in this hope, and, indignant, alarmed almost, at the prospect of a lonesome evening under these circumstances, she ran hastily down to the gate to meet him, crying:

"Oh, Ned, you look so troubled I know you have only come home for a hurried supper. But you cannot leave me to-night. Tennie" (their only maid) "has gone for a holiday, and I never can stay in this house alone with all that." She pointed to the small bag he carried, which, as she knew, was filled to bursting with bank notes.

He certainly looked troubled. It is hard to resist the entreaty in a young bride's uplifted face. But this time he could not help himself, and he said:

"I am dreadful sorry, but I must ride over to Fairbanks to-night. Mr. Pierson has given me an imperative order to conclude a matter of business there, and it is very important that it should be done. I should lose my position if I neglected the matter, and no one but Hasbrouck and Suffern knows that we keep the money in the house. I have always given out that I intrusted it to Hale's safe over night."

"But I cannot stand it," she persisted. "You have never left me on these nights. That is why I let Tennie go. I will spend the evening at The Larches, or, better still, call in Mr. and Mrs. Talcott to keep me company."

But her husband did not approve of her going out or of her having company. The Larches was too far away, and as for Mr. and Mrs. Talcott, they were meddlesome people, whom he had never liked; besides, Mrs. Talcott was delicate, and the night threatened storm. It seemed hard to subject her to this ordeal, and he showed that he thought so by his manner, but, as circumstances were, she would have to stay alone, and he only hoped she would be brave and go to bed like a good girl, and think nothing about the money, which he would take care to put away in a very safe place.

"Or," said he, kissing her downcast face, "perhaps you would rather hide it yourself; women always have curious ideas about such things."

"Yes, let me hide it," she murmured. "The money, I mean, not the bag. Every one knows the bag. I should never dare to leave it in that." And begging him to unlock it, she began to empty it with a feverish haste that rather alarmed him, for he surveyed her anxiously and shook his head as if he dreaded the effects of this excitement upon her.

But as he saw no way of averting it he confined himself to using such soothing words as were at his command, and then, humoring her weakness, helped her to arrange the bills in the place she had chosen, and restuffing the bag with old receipts till it acquired its former dimensions, he put a few bills on top to make the whole look natural, and, laughing at her white face, relocked the bag and put the key back in his pocket.

"There, dear; a notable scheme and one that should relieve your mind entirely!" he cried. "If any one should attempt burglary in my absence and should succeed in getting into a house as safely locked as this will be when I leave it, then trust to their being satisfied when they see this booty, which I shall hide where I always hide it—in the cupboard over my desk."

"And when will you be back?" she murmured, trembling in spite of herself at these preparations.

"By one o'clock if possible. Certainly by two."

"And our neighbors go to bed at ten," she murmured. But the words were low, and she was glad he did not hear them, for if it was his duty to obey the orders he had received, then it was her duty to meet the position in which it left her as bravely as she could.

At supper she was so natural that his face rapidly brightened, and it was with quite an air of cheerfulness that he rose at last to lock up the house and make such preparations as were necessary for his dismal ride over the mountains to Fairbanks. She had the supper dishes to wash up in Tennie's absence, and as she was a busy little housewife she found herself singing a snatch of song as she passed back and forth from dining-room to kitchen. He heard it, too, and smiled to himself as he bolted the windows on the ground floor and examined the locks of the three lower doors, and when he finally came into the kitchen with his great-coat on to give her his final kiss, he had but one parting injunction to urge, and that was that she should lock the front door after him and then forget the whole matter till she heard his double knock at midnight.

She smiled and held up her ingenuous face.

"Be careful of yourself," she murmured. "I hate this dark ride for you, and on such a night too." And she ran with him to the door to look out.

"It is certainly very dark," he responded, "but I'm to have one of Brown's safest horses. Do not worry about me. I shall do well enough, and so will you, too, or you are not the plucky little woman I have always thought you."

She laughed, but there was a choking sound in her voice that made him look at her again. But at sight of his anxiety she recovered herself, and pointing to the clouds said earnestly:

"It is going to snow. Be careful as you ride by the gorge, Ned; it is very deceptive there in a snowstorm."

But he vowed that it would not snow before morning, and giving her one final embrace he dashed down the path toward Brown's livery stable. "Oh, what is the matter with me?" she murmured to herself as his steps died out in the distance. "I never knew I was such a coward." And she paused for a moment, looking up and down the road, as if in despite of her husband's command she had the desperate idea of running away to some neighbor.

But she was too loyal for that, and smothering a sigh she retreated into the house. As she did so the first flakes fell of the storm that was not to have come till morning.

It took her an hour to get her kitchen in order, and nine o'clock struck before she was ready to sit down. She had been so busy she had not noticed how the wind had increased or how rapidly the snow was falling. But when she went to the front door for another glance up and down the road she started back, appalled at the fierceness of the gale and at the great pile of snow that had already accumulated on the doorstep.

Too delicate to breast such a wind, she saw herself robbed of her last hope of any companionship, and sighing heavily she locked and bolted the door for the night and went back into her little sitting-room, where a great fire was burning. Here she sat down, and determined, now that she must pass the evening alone, to do it as cheerfully as possible, and so began to sew. "Oh, what a Christmas eve!" she thought, and a picture of other homes rose before her eyes, homes in which husbands sat by wives and brothers by sisters, and a great wave of regret poured over her and a longing for something, she hardly dared say what, lest her unhappiness should acquire a sting that would leave traces beyond the passing moment.

The room in which she sat was the only one on the ground floor except the dining-room and kitchen. It therefore was used both as parlor and sitting-room, and held not only her piano, but her husband's desk.

Communicating with it was the tiny dining-room. Between the two, however, was an entry leading to a side entrance. A lamp was in this entry, and she had left it burning, as well as the one in the kitchen, that the house might look cheerful and as if all the family were at home.

She was looking toward this entry and wondering whether it was the mist made by her tears that made it look so dismally dark to her when there came a faint sound from the door at its further end.

Knowing that her husband must have taken peculiar pains with the fastenings of this door, as it was the one toward the woods and therefore most accessible to wayfarers, she sat where she was, with all her faculties strained to listen. But no further sound came from that direction, and after a few minutes of silent terror she was allowing herself to believe that she had been deceived by her fears when she suddenly heard the same sound at the kitchen door, followed by a muffled knock.

Frightened now in good earnest, but still alive to the fact that the intruder was as likely to be a friend as a foe, she stepped to the door, and with her hand on the lock stooped and asked boldly enough who was there. But she received no answer, and more affected by this unexpected silence than by the knock she had heard she recoiled farther and farther till not only the width of the kitchen, but the dining-room also, lay between her and the scene of her alarm, when to her utter confusion the noise shifted again to the side of the house, and the door she thought so securely fastened, swung violently open as if blown in by a fierce gust, and she saw precipitated into the entry the burly figure of a man covered with snow and shaking with the violence of the storm that seemed at once to fill the house.

Her first thought was that it was her husband come back, but before she could clear her eyes from the cloud of snow which had entered with him he had thrown off his outer covering and she found herself face to face with a man in whose powerful frame and cynical visage she saw little to comfort her and much to surprise and alarm.

"Ugh!" was his coarse and rather familiar greeting. "A hard night, missus! Enough to drive any man indoors. Pardon the liberty, but I couldn't wait for you to lift the latch; the wind drove me right in."

"Was—was not the door locked?" she feebly asked, thinking he must have staved it in with his foot, that looked only too well fitted for such a task.

"Not much," he chuckled. "I s'pose you're too hospitable for that." And his eyes passed from her face to the comfortable firelight shining through the sitting-room.

"Is it refuge you want?" she demanded, suppressing as much as possible all signs of fear.

"Sure, missus—what else! A man can't live in a gale like that, specially after a tramp of twenty miles or more. Shall I shut the door for you?" he asked, with a mixture of bravado and good nature that frightened her more and more.

"I will shut it," she replied, with a half notion of escaping this sinister stranger by a flight through the night.

But one glance into the swirling snow-storm deterred her, and making the best of the alarming situation, she closed the door, but did not lock it, being more afraid now of what was inside the house than of anything left to threaten her from without.

The man, whose clothes were dripping with water, watched her with a cynical smile, and then, without any invitation, entered the dining-room, crossed it and moved toward the kitchen fire.

"Ugh! ugh! But it is warm here!" he cried, his nostrils dilating with an animal-like enjoyment that in itself was repugnant to her womanly delicacy. "Do you know, missus, I shall have to stay here all night? Can't go out in that gale again; not such a fool." Then with a sly look at her trembling form and white face he insinuatingly added, "All alone, missus?"

The suddenness with which this was put, together with the leer that accompanied it, made her start. Alone? Yes, but should she acknowledge it? Would it not be better to say that her husband was up-stairs. The man evidently saw the struggle going on in her mind, for he chuckled to himself and called out quite boldly:

"Never mind, missus; it's all right. Just give me a bit of cold meat and a cup of tea or something, and we'll be very comfortable together. You're a slender slip of a woman to be minding a house like this. I'll keep you company if you don't mind, leastwise until the storm lets up a bit, which ain't likely for some hours to come. Rough night, missus, rough night."

"I expect my husband home at any time," she hastened to say. And thinking she saw a change in the man's countenance at this she put on quite an air of sudden satisfaction and bounded toward the front of the house. "There! I think I hear him now," she cried.

Her motive was to gain time, and if possible to obtain the opportunity of shifting the money from the place where she had first put it into another and safer one. "I want to be able," she thought, "of swearing that I have no money with me in this house. If I can only get it into my apron I will drop it outside the door into the snowbank. It will be as safe there as in the bank it came from." And dashing into the sitting-room she made a feint of dragging down a shawl from a screen, while she secretly filled her skirt with the bills which had been put between some old pamphlets on the book-shelves.

She could hear the man grumbling in the kitchen, but he did not follow her front, and taking advantage of the moment's respite from his none too encouraging presence she unbarred the door and cheerfully called out her husband's name.

The ruse was successful. She was enabled

to fling the notes where the falling flakes would soon cover them from sight, and feeling more courageous, now that the money was out of the house, she went slowly back, saying she had made a mistake, and that it was the wind she had heard.

The man gave a gruff but knowing guffaw and then resumed his watch over her, following her steps as she proceeded to set him out a meal, with a persistency that reminded her of a tiger just on the point of springing. But the inviting look of the viands with which she was rapidly setting the table soon distracted his attention, and allowing himself one grunt of satisfaction, he drew up a chair and set himself down to what to him was evidently a most savory repast.

"No beer? No ale? Nothing o' that sort, eh? Don't keep a bar?" he growled, as his teeth closed on a huge hunk of bread.

She shook her head, wishing she had a little cold poison bottled up in a tight-looking jug.

"Nothing but tea," she smiled, astonished at her own ease of manner in the presence of this alarming guest.

"Then let's have that," he grumbled, taking the bowl she handed him, with an odd look that made her glad to retreat to the other side of the room.

"Jest listen to the howling wind," he went on between the huge mouthfuls of bread and cheese with which he was gorging himself. "But we're very comfortable, we two! We don't mind the storm, do we?"

Shocked by his familiarity and still more moved by the look of mingled inquiry and curiosity with which his eyes now began to wander over the walls and cupboards, she took an anxious step toward the side of the house looking toward her neighbors, and lifting one of the shades, which had all been religiously pulled down, she looked out. A swirl of snow-flakes alone confronted her. She could neither see her neighbors, nor could she be seen by them. A shout from her to them would not be heard. She was as completely isolated as if the house stood in the center of a desolate western plain.

"I have no trust but in God," she murmured as she came from the window. And, nerved to meet her fate, she crossed to the kitchen.

It was now half-past ten. Two hours and a half must elapse before her husband could possibly arrive.

She set her teeth at the thought and walked resolutely into the room.

"Are you done?" she asked.

"I am, ma'am," he leered. "Do you want me to wash the dishes? I kin, and I will." And he actually carried his plate and cup to the sink, where he turned the water upon them with another loud guffaw.

"If only his fancy would take him into the pantry," she thought, "I could shut and lock the door upon him and hold him prisoner till Ned gets back."

But his fancy ended its flight at the sink, and before her hopes had fully subsided he was standing on the threshold of the sitting-room door.

"It's pretty here," he exclaimed, allowing his eye to rove again over every hiding-place within sight. "I wonder now"— He stopped. His glance had fallen on the cupboard over her husband's desk.

"Well?" she asked, anxious to break the thread of his thought, which was only too plainly mirrored in his eager countenance.

He started, dropped his eyes, and turning looked at her with a momentary fierceness. But, as she did not let her own glance quail, but continued to look at him with what she meant for a smile on her pale lips, he subdued this outward manifestation of passion, and, chuckling to hide his embarrassment, began backing into the entry, leering in evident enjoyment of the fears he caused, with what she felt was a most horrible smile. Once in the hall, he hesitated, however, for a long time; then he slowly went toward the garment he had dropped on entering and stooping, drew from underneath its folds a wicked-looking stick. Giving a kick to the coat, which sent it into a remote corner, he bestowed upon her another smile, and still carrying the stick went slowly and reluctantly away into the kitchen.

"Oh, God Almighty, help me!" was her prayer.

There was nothing for her to do now but endure, so throwing herself into a chair, she tried to calm the beating of her heart and summon up courage for the struggle which she felt was before her. That he had come to rob and only waited to take her off her guard she now felt certain, and rapidly running over in her mind all the expedients of self-defense possible to one in her situation, she suddenly remembered the pistol which Ned kept in his desk. Oh, why had she not thought of it before! Why had she let herself grow mad with terror when here, within reach of her hand, lay such a means of self-defense? With a feeling of joy (she had always hated pistols before and scolded Ned when he bought this one) she started to her feet and slid her hand into the drawer. But it came back empty. Ned had taken the weapon away with him.

For a moment, a surge of the bitterest feeling she had ever experienced passed over her; then she called reason to her aid and was obliged to acknowledge that the act was but natural, and that from his standpoint he was much more likely to need it than herself. But the disappointment, coming so soon after hope, unnerved her, and she sank back in her chair, giving herself up for lost.

How long she sat there with her eyes on the door, through which she momentarily expected her assailant to reappear, she never knew. She was conscious only of a sort of apathy that made movement difficult and even breathing a task. In vain she tried to change her thoughts. In vain she tried to follow her husband in fancy over the snow-covered roads and into the gorge of the mountains. Imagination failed her at this point. Do what she would, all was misty in her mind's eye, and she could not see that wandering image. There was blankness between his form and her, and no life or movement anywhere but here in the scene of her terror.

Her eyes were on a strip of rug that covered the entry floor, and so strange was the condition of her mind that she found herself mechanically counting the tassels that finished its edge, growing wroth over one that was worn, till she hated that sixth tassel and mentally determined that if she ever outlived this night she would strip them all off and be done with them.

The wind had lessened, but the air had grown cooler and the snow made a sharp sound where it struck the panes. She felt it falling, though she had cut off all view of it. It seemed to her that a pall was settling over the world and that she would soon be smothered under its folds. Meanwhile no sound came from the kitchen, only that dreadful sense of a doom creeping upon her—a sense that grew in intensity till she found herself watching for the shadow of that lifted stick on the wall of the entry, and almost imagined she saw the tip of it appearing, when without any premonition, that fatal side door again blew in and admitted another man of so threatening an aspect that she succumbed instantly before him and forgot all her former fears in this new terror.

The second intruder was a negro of powerful frame and lowering aspect, and as he came forward and stood in the doorway there was observable in his fierce and desperate countenance no attempt at the insinuation of the other, only a fearful resolution that made her feel like a puppet before him, and drove her, almost without her volition, to her knees.

"Money? Is it money you want?" was her desperate greeting. "If so, here's my purse and here are my rings and watch. Take them and go."

But the stolid wretch did not even stretch out his hands. His eyes went beyond her, and the mingled anxiety and resolve which he displayed would have cowed a stouter heart than that of this poor woman.

"Keep de trash," he growled. "I want de company's money. You 've got it—two thousand dollars. Show me where it is, that's all, and I won't trouble you long after I close on it."

"But it's not in the house," she cried. "I swear it is not in the house. Do you think Mr. Chivers would leave me here alone with two thousand dollars to guard?"

But the negro, swearing that she lied, leaped into the room, and tearing open the cupboard above her husband's desk, seized the bag from the corner where they had put it.

"He brought it in this," he muttered, and tried to force the bag open, but finding this impossible he took out a heavy knife and cut a big hole in its side. Instantly there fell out the pile of old receipts with which they had stuffed it, and seeing these he stamped with rage, and flinging them in one great handful at her rushed to the drawers below, emptied them, and, finding nothing, attacked the bookcase.

"The money is somewhere here. You can't

fool me," he yelled. "I saw the spot your eyes lit on when I first came into the room. Is it behind these books?" he growled, pulling them out and throwing them helter-skelter over the floor. "Women is smart in the hiding business. Is it behind these books, I say?"

They had been, or rather had been placed between the books, but she had taken them away, as we know, and he soon began to realize that his search was bringing him nothing, for leaving the bookcase he gave the books one kick, and seizing her by the arm, shook her with a murderous glare on his strange and distorted features.

"Where's the money?" he hissed. "Tell me, or you are a goner."

He raised his heavy fist. She crouched and all seemed over, when, with a rush and cry, a figure dashed between them and he fell, struck down by the very stick she had so long been expecting to see fall upon her own head. The man who had been her terror for hours had at the moment of need acted as her protector.

* * * * *

She must have fainted, but if so, her unconsciousness was but momentary, for when she again recognized her surroundings she found the tramp still standing over her adversary.

"I hope you don't mind, ma'am," he said, with an air of humbleness she certainly had not seen in him before, "but I think the man's dead." And he stirred with his foot the heavy figure before him.

"Oh, no, no, no!" she cried. "That would be too fearful. He's shocked, stunned; you cannot have killed him."

But the tramp was persistent. "I'm 'fraid I have," he said. "I done it before, and it's been the same every time. But I couldn't see a man of that color frighten a lady like you. My supper was too warm in me, ma'am. Shall I throw him outside the house?"

"Yes," she said, and then, "No; let us first be sure there is no life in him." And, hardly knowing what she did, she stooped down and peered into the glassy eyes of the prostrate man.

Suddenly she turned pale--no, not pale, but ghastly, and cowering back, shook so that the tramp, into whose features a certain refinement had passed since he had acted as her protector, thought she had discovered life in those set orbs, and was stooping down to make sure that this was so, when he saw her suddenly lean forward and, impetuously plunging her hand into the negro's throat, tear open the shirt and give one look at his bared breast.

It was white.

"O God! O God!" she moaned, and lifting the head in her two hands she gave the motionless features a long and searching look. "Water!" she cried. "Bring water." But before the now obedient tramp could respond, she had torn off the woolly wig disfiguring the dead man's head, and seeing the blond curls beneath had uttered such a shriek that it rose above the gale and was heard by her distant neighbors.

It was the head and hair of her husband.

* * * * *

They found out afterwards that he had contemplated this theft for months, that each and every precaution possible to a successful issue to this most daring undertaking had been made use of and that but for the unexpected presence in the house of the tramp, he would doubtless have not only extorted the money from his wife, but have so covered up the deed by a plausible *alibi* as to have retained her confidence and that of his employers.

Whether the tramp killed him out of sympathy for the defenseless woman or in rage at being disappointed in his own plans has never been determined. Mrs. Chivers herself thinks he was actuated by a rude sort of gratitude.

THE STAIRCASE AT THE HEART'S DELIGHT

THE STAIRCASE AT THE HEART'S DELIGHT.[1]

AS TOLD BY MR. GRYCE.

"IN the spring of 1840, the attention of the New York police was attracted by the many cases of well-known men found drowned in the various waters surrounding the lower portion of our great city. Among these may be mentioned the name of Elwood Henderson, the noted tea merchant, whose remains were washed ashore at Redhook Point; and of Christopher Bigelow, who was picked up off Governor's Island after having been in the water for five days, and of another well-known millionaire whose name I cannot now recall, but who, I remember, was seen to walk towards the East River one March evening, and was not met with again till the 5th of April, when his body floated into one of the docks near Peck Slip.

"As it seemed highly improbable that there should have been a concerted action among so many wealthy and distinguished men to end their lives within a few weeks of each other, and all by the same method of drowning, we soon became suspicious that a more serious verdict than that of suicide should have been rendered in the case of Henderson, Bigelow and the other gentleman I have mentioned. Yet one fact, common to all these cases, pointed so conclusively to deliberate intention on the part of the sufferers that we hesitated to take action.

"This was, that upon the body of each of the above-mentioned persons there were found, not only valuables in the shape of money and jewelry, but papers and memoranda of a nature calculated to fix the identity of the drowned man, in case the water should rob him of his personal characteristics. Consequently, we could not ascribe these deaths to a desire for plunder on the part of some unknown person.

"I was a young man in those days, and full of ambition. So, though I said nothing, I did not let this matter drop when the others did, but kept my mind persistently upon it and waited, with odd results as you will hear, for another victim to be reported at police head-quarters.

"Meantime I sought to discover some bond or connection between the several men who had been found drowned, which would serve to explain their similar fate. But all my efforts in this direction were fruitless. There was no bond between them, and the matter remained for a while an unsolved mystery.

"Suddenly one morning a clew was placed, not in my hands, but in those of a superior official who at that time exerted a great influence over the whole force. He was sitting in his private room, when there was ushered into his presence a young man of a dissipated but not unprepossessing appearance, who, after a pause of marked embarrassment, entered upon the following story:

"I don't know whether or no, I should offer an excuse for the communication I am about to make; but the matter I have to relate is simply this: Being hard up last night (for though a rich man's son I often lack money), I went to a certain pawn-shop in the Bowery where I had been told I could raise money on my prospects. This place—you may see it some time, so I will not enlarge upon it—did not strike me favorably; but, being very anxious for a certain definite sum of money, I wrote my name in a book which was brought to me from some unknown quarter, and proceeded to follow the young woman who attended me into what she was pleased to call her good master's private office. He may have been a good master, but he was anything but a good man. In short, sir, when he found out who I was, and how much I needed money, he suggested that I should make an appointment with my father at a place he called Judah's in Grand

Street, where, said he, 'your little affair will be arranged, and you made a rich man within thirty days. That is,' he slyly added, 'unless your father has already made a will, disinheriting you.'

"I was shocked, sir, shocked beyond all my powers of concealment, not so much at his words, which I hardly understood, as at his looks, which had a world of evil suggestion in them; so I raised my fist and would have knocked him down, only that I found two young fellows at my elbows, who held me quiet for five minutes, while the old fellow talked to me. He asked me if I came to him on a fool's errand or really to get money; and when I admitted that I had cherished hopes of obtaining a clear two thousand dollars from him, he coolly replied that he knew of but one way in which I could hope to get such an amount, and that if I was too squeamish to adopt it, I had made a mistake in coming to his shop, which was no missionary institution, etc., etc. Not wishing to irritate him, for there was menace in his eye, I asked, with a certain weak show of being sorry for my former heat, whereabouts in Grand Street I should find this Judah. The retort was quick, 'Judah is not his name,' said he, 'and Grand Street is not where you are to go to find him. I threw out a bait to see if you would snap at it, but I find you timid, and therefore advise you to drop the matter entirely.' I was quite willing to do so, and answered him to this effect; whereupon, with a side glance I did not understand but which made me more or less uneasy in regard to his intentions towards me, he motioned to the men who held my arms to let go their hold, which they at once did.

"'We have your signature,' growled the old man as I went out. 'If you peach on us or trouble us in any way we will show it to your father and that will put an end to all your hopes of future fortune.' Then raising his voice he shouted to the girl in the outer office, 'Let the young man see what he has signed.' She smiled and again brought forward the book in which I had so recklessly placed my name, and there at the top of the page I read these words: 'For moneys received, I agree to notify Levi Solomon, within the month, of the death of my father, that he may recover from me, without loss of time, the sum of ten thousand dollars from the amount I am bound to receive as my father's heir.' The sight of these lines knocked me hollow. But I am less of a coward morally than physically, and I determined to acquaint my father at once with what I had done, and get his advice as to whether or not I should inform the police of my adventure. He heard me with more consideration than I expected, but insisted that I should immediately make known to you my experience in this Bowery pawnbroker's shop.

"The officer, highly interested, took down the young man's statement in writing, and, after getting a more accurate description of the Jew's house, allowed his visitor to go.

"Fortunately for me I was in the building

at the time, and was able to respond when a man was called up to investigate this matter. Thinking that I saw a connection between it and the various mysterious deaths of which I have previously spoken, I entered into the affair with much spirit. But, wishing to be sure that my possibly unwarranted conclusions were correct, I took pains to inquire, before proceeding upon my errand, into the character of the heirs who had inherited the property of Elwood Henderson and Christopher Bigelow, and found that in each case there was one among the rest who was well known for his profligacy and reckless expenditure. It was a significant discovery, and increased, if possible, my interest in running down this nefarious trafficker in the lives of wealthy men.

"Knowing that I could hope for no success in my character of detective, I made an arrangement with the father of the young gentleman before alluded to, by which I was to enter the pawn-shop as an emissary of the latter. I accordingly appeared there, one dull

November afternoon, in the garb of a certain western sporting man, who, for a consideration, allowed me the temporary use of his name and credentials.

" Entering beneath the three golden balls, with the swagger and general air of ownership I thought most likely to impose upon the self-satisfied female who presided over the desk, I asked to see her boss.

" 'On your own business?' she queried, glancing with suspicion at my short coat, which was rather more showy than elegant.

" 'No,' I returned, 'not on my own business, but on that of a young gent——'

" 'Anyone whose name is written here?' she interposed, reaching towards me the famous book, over the top of which, however, she was careful to lay her arm.

" I glanced down the page she had opened and instantly detected that of the young gentleman on whose behalf I was supposed to be there, and nodded 'Yes,' with all the assurance of which I was capable.

"'Very well, then,' said she, 'come!' and she ushered me without much ado into a den of discomfort where sat a man, with a great beard and such heavy overhanging eyebrows that I could hardly detect the twinkle of his eyes, keen and incisive as they were.

"Smiling upon him, but not in the same way I had upon the girl, I glanced behind me at the open door, and above me at the partitions, which failed to reach the ceiling. Then I shook my head and drew a step nearer.

"'I have come,' I insinuatingly whispered, 'on behalf of a certain party who left this place in a huff a day or so ago, but who since then has had time to think the matter over, and has sent me with an apology which he hopes'— here I put on a diabolical smile, copied, I declare to you, from the one I saw at that moment on his own lips—'you will accept.'

"The old wretch regarded me for full two minutes in a way to unmask me had I possessed less confidence in my disguise and in my ability to support it.

"'And what is this young gentleman's name?' he finally asked.

"For reply, I handed him a slip of paper. He took it and read the few lines written on it, after which he began to rub his palms together with a snaky unction eminently in keeping with the stray glints of light that now and then found their way through his bushy eyebrows.

"'And so the young gentleman had not the courage to come again himself?' he softly suggested, with just the suspicion of an ironical laugh. 'Thought, perhaps, I would exact too much commission; or make him pay too roundly for his impertinent assurance.'

"I shrugged my shoulders, but vouchsafed no immediate reply, and he saw that he had to open the business himself. He did it warily and with many an incisive question which would have tripped me up if I had not been very much on my guard; but it all ended, as such matters usually do, in mutual understanding, and a promise that if the young gentleman was willing to sign a certain paper, which, by the way, was not shown me, he would in exchange give him an address which, if made proper use of, would lead to my patron finding himself an independent man within a very few days.

"As this address was the thing above all others which I most desired, I professed myself satisfied with the arrangement, and proceeded to hunt up my patron, as he was called. Informing him of the result of my visit, I asked if his interest in ferreting out these criminals was strong enough to lead him to sign the vile document which the Jew would probably have in readiness for him on the morrow; and being told it was, we separated for that day, with the understanding that we were to meet the next morning at the spot chosen by the Jew for the completion of his nefarious bargain.

"Being certain that I was being followed in all my movements by the agents of this adept in villainy, I took care, upon leaving Mr. L——, to repair to the hotel of the sporting man I was personifying. Making myself square with the proprietor, I took up my quarters in the room of my sporting friend, and, the better to deceive any spy who might be lurking about, I received his letters and sent out his telegrams, which, if they did not create confusion in the affairs of 'The Plunger,' must at least have occasioned him no little work the next day.

"Promptly at ten o'clock on the following morning I met my patron at the place of rendezvous appointed by the old Jew; and when I tell you that this was no other than the old cemetery of which a portion is still to be seen off Chatham Square, you will understand the uncanny nature of this whole adventure, and the lurking sense there was in it of brooding death and horror. The scene, which in these days is disturbed by elevated railroad trains and the flapping of long lines of parti-colored clothes strung high up across the quiet tombstones, was at that time one of peaceful rest, in the midst of a quarter devoted to everything for which that rest is the fitting and desirable end; and as we paused among the mossy stones, we found it hard to realize that in a few minutes there would be standing beside us the concentrated essence of all that was evil and despicable in human nature.

"He arrived with a smile on his countenance that completed his ugliness, and would have frightened any honest man from his side at once. Merely glancing my way, he shuffled up to my companion, and leading him aside, drew out a paper which he laid on a flat tombstone with a gesture significant of his desire that the other should affix to it the required signature.

"Meantime I stood guard, and while attempting to whistle a light air, was carelessly taking in the surroundings, and conjecturing, as best I might, the reasons which had induced the old ghoul to make use of this spot for his diabolical business, and had about decided that it was because he was a ghoul, and thus felt at home among the symbols of mortality, when I caught sight of two or three young fellows, who were lounging on the other side of the fence.

"These were so evidently accomplices that I wondered if the two sly boys I had engaged to stand by me through this affair had spotted them, and would know enough to follow them back to their haunts.

"A few minutes later, the old rascal came sneaking towards me, with a gleam of satisfaction in his half-closed eyes.

"'You are not wanted any longer,' he grunted. 'The young gentleman told me to say that he could look out for himself now.'

"'The young gentleman had better pay me the round fifty he promised me,' I grumbled in return, with that sudden change from indifference to menace which I thought best calculated to further my plans; and shouldering the miserable wretch aside, I stepped up to my companion, who was still lingering in a state of hesitation among the gravestones.

"'Quick! Tell me the number and street which he has given you!' I whispered, in a tone strangely in contrast with the angry and reproachful air I had assumed.

"He was about to answer, when the old fellow came sidling up behind us. Instantly the young man before me rose to the occasion, and putting on an air of conciliation said in a soothing tone:

"'There, there, don't bluster. Do one thing more for me, and I will add another fifty to those I promised you. Conjure up an anonymous letter—you know how—and send it to my father, saying that if he wants to know where his son loses his hundreds, he must go to the place on the dock, opposite 5 South Street, some night shortly after nine. It would not work with most men, but it will with my father, and when he has been in and out of that place, and I succeed to the fortune he will leave me, then I will remember you, and——'

"'Say, too,' a sinister voice here added in my ear, 'that if he wishes to effect an entrance into the gambling den which his son haunts, he must take the precaution of tying a bit of blue ribbon in his button-hole. It is a signal meaning business, and must not be forgotten,' chuckled the old fellow, evidently deceived at last into thinking I was really one of his own kind.

"I answered by a wink, and taking care to attempt no further communication with my patron, I left the two, as soon as possible, and went back to the hotel, where I dropped 'the sport,' and assumed a character and dress which enabled me to make my way undetected to the house of my young patron, where for two days I lay low, waiting for a suitable time in which to make my final attempt to penetrate this mystery.

"I knew that for the adventure I was now contemplating considerable courage was required. But I did not hesitate. The time had come for me to show my mettle. In the few communications I was enabled to hold with my superiors I told them of my progress and arranged with them my plan of work. As we all agreed that I was about to encounter no common villainy, these plans naturally partook of finesse, as you will see if you will follow my narrative to the end.

"Early in the evening of a cool November night I sallied forth into the streets, dressed in the habiliments and wearing the guise of the wealthy old gentleman whose secret guest I had been for the last few days. As he was old and portly, and I young and spare, this disguise had cost me no little thought and labor. But assisted as I was by the darkness, I had but little fear of betraying myself to any chance spy who might be upon the watch, especially as Mr. L—— had a peculiar walk, which, in my short stay with him, I had learned to imitate perfectly. In the lapel of my overcoat I had tied a tag of blue ribbon, and, though for all I knew this was a signal devoting me to a secret and mysterious death, I walked along in a buoyant condition of mind, attributable, no doubt, to the excitement of the venture and to my desire to test my powers, even at the risk of my life.

"It was nine o'clock when I reached South Street. It was no new region to me, nor was I ignorant of the specified drinking den on the dock to which I had been directed. I remembered it as a bright spot in a mass of ship-prows and bow-rigging, and was possessed, besides, of a vague consciousness that there was something odd in connection with it which had aroused my curiosity sufficiently in the past for me to have once formed the resolution of seeing it again under circumstances which would allow me to give it some attention. But I never thought that the circumstances would involve my own life, impossible as it is for a detective to reckon upon the future or to foresee the events into which he will be hurried by the next crime which may be reported at police headquarters.

"There were but few persons in the street when I crossed to The Heart's Delight,—so named from the heart-shaped opening in the framework of the door, through which shone a light, inviting enough to one chilled by the keen November air and oppressed by the desolate appearance of the almost deserted street. But amongst those persons I thought I recognized more than one familiar form, and felt reassured as to the watch which had been set upon the house. The night was dark and the river especially so, but in the gloomy space beyond the dock I detected a shadow blacker than the rest, which I took for the police-boat they had promised to have in readiness in case I needed rescue from the water-side. Otherwise the surroundings were as usual, and saving the gruff singing of some drunken sailor coming from a narrow side street near by, no sound disturbed the somewhat lugubrious silence of this weird and forsaken spot.

"Pausing an instant before entering, I glanced up at the building, which was about three stories high, and endeavored to see what there was about it which had once arrested my attention, and came to the conclusion that it was its exceptional situation on the dock, and the ghostly effect of the hoisting-beam projecting from the upper story like a gibbet. And yet this beam was common to many a warehouse in the vicinity, though in none of them were there any such signs of life as proceeded from the curious mixture of sail loft, boat shop and drinking saloon, now before me. Could it be that the ban of criminality was upon the house, and that I had been conscious of this without being able to realize the cause of my interest?

"Not stopping to solve my sensations further, I tried the door, and, finding it yield easily to my touch, turned the knob and entered. For a moment I was blinded by the smoky glare of the heated atmosphere into which I stepped, but presently I was able to distinguish the vague outlines of an oyster bar in the distance, and the motionless figures of some half dozen men, whose movements had been arrested by my sudden entrance. For an instant this picture remained ; then the drinking and card-playing were resumed, and I stood, as it were, alone on the sanded floor near the door. Improving the opportunity for a closer inspection of the place, I was struck by its picturesqueness. It had evidently been once used as a ship chandlery, and on the walls, which were but partly plastered, there still hung old bits of marlin, rusty rings and such other evidences of former traffic as did not interfere with the present more lucrative business.

"Below were the two bars, one at the right of the door, and the other at the lower end of the room near a window, through whose small, square panes I caught a glimpse of the colored lights of a couple of ferry boats, passing each other in midstream.

"At a table near me sat two men, grumbling

at each other over a game of cards. They were large and powerful figures in the contracted space of this long and narrow room, and my heart gave a bound of joy as I recognized on them certain marks by which I was to know friend from foe in this possible den of thieves and murderers.

"Two sailors at the bar were *bona fide* habitués of the place, and so I judged to be the one or two other specimens of water-side character whose backs I could faintly discern in one of the dim corners. Meantime a man was approaching me.

"Let me see if I can describe him. He was about thirty, and had the complexion and figure of a consumptive, but his eye shone with the yellow glare of a beast of prey, and in the cadaverous hollows of his ashen cheeks and amid the lines about his thin drawn lips there lay for all his conciliatory smile, an expression so cold and yet so ferocious that I spotted him at once as the man to whose genius we were indebted for the new scheme of murder which

I was jeopardizing my life to understand. But I allowed none of the repugnance with which he inspired me to appear in my manner, and, greeting him with half a nod, waited for him to speak. His voice had that smooth quality which betrays the hypocrite.

"'Has the gentleman an appointment here?' he asked, letting his glance fall for the merest instant on the lapel of my coat.

"I returned a decided affirmative. 'Or rather,' I went on, with a meaning look he evidently comprehended, 'my son has, and I have made up my mind to know just what deviltry he is up to these days. 'You see I can make it worth your while to give me the opportunity.'

'O, I see,' he assented with a glance at the pocketbook I had just drawn out. 'You want a private room from which you can watch the young scapegrace. I understand, I understand. But the private rooms are above. Gentlemen are not comfortable here.'

"'I should say not,' I murmured, and drew

from the pocketbook a bill which I slid quietly into his hand. 'Now take me where I shall be safe,' I suggested, 'and yet in full sight of the room where the young gentlemen play. I wish to catch him at his tricks. Afterwards——'

"'All will be well,' he finished smoothly, with another glance at my blue ribbon. 'You see I do not ask you the young gentleman's name. I take your money and leave all the rest to you. Only don't make a scandal, I pray, for my house has the name of being quiet.'

"'Yes,' thought I, 'too quiet!' and for an instant felt my spirits fail me. But it was only for an instant. I had friends about me and a pistol at half cock in the pocket of my overcoat. Why should I fear any surprise, prepared as I was for every emergency?

"'I will show you up in a moment,' said he; and left me to put up a heavy board-shutter over the window opening on the river. Was this a signal or a precaution? I glanced towards my two friends playing cards, took another note of their broad shoulders and brawny arms, and prepared to follow my host, who now stood bowing at the other end of the room, before a covered staircase which was manifestly the sole means of reaching the floor above.

"The staircase was quite a feature in the room. It ran from back to front, and was boarded all the way up to the ceiling. On these boards hung a few useless bits of chain, wire and knotted ends of tarred ropes, which swung to and fro as the sharp November blast struck the building, giving out a weird and strangely muffled sound. Why did this sound, so easily to be accounted for, ring in my ears like a note of warning? I understand now, but I did not then, full of expectation as I was for developments out of the ordinary.

"Crossing the room, I entered upon the staircase, in the wake of my companion. Though the two men at cards did not look up as I passed them, I noticed that they were alert and ready for any signal I might choose to give them. But I was not ready to give one yet. I must see danger before I summoned help, and there was no token of danger yet.

"When we were about half-way up the stairs the faint light which had illuminated us from below suddenly vanished, and we found ourselves in total darkness. The door at the foot had been closed by a careful hand, and I felt, rather than heard, the stealthy pushing of a bolt across it.

"My first impulse was to forsake my guide and rush back, but I subdued the unworthy impulse and stood quite still, while my companion exclaiming, 'Damn that fellow! What does he mean by shutting the door before we're half-way up!' struck a match and lit a gas jet in the room above, which poured a flood of light upon the staircase. Drawing my hand from the pocket in which I had put my revolver, I hastened after him into the small landing at the top of the stairs. An open door was before me, in which he stood bowing, with the half-burnt match in his hand. 'This is the place, sir,' he announced, motioning me in.

"I entered and he remained by the door, while I passed quickly about the room, which was bare of every article of furniture save a solitary table and chair. There was not even a window in it, with the exception of one small light situated so high up in the corner made by the jutting-up staircase that I wondered at its use, and was only relieved of extreme apprehension at the prison-like appearance of the place by the gleam of light which came through this dusty pane, showing that I was not entirely removed from the presence of my foes if I was from that of my friends.

"'Ah, you have spied the window,' remarked my host, advancing toward me with a countenance he vainly endeavored to make reassuring and friendly. 'That is your post of observation, sir,' he whispered, with a great show of mystery. 'By mounting on the table you can peer into the room where my young friends sit securely at play.'

" As it was not part of my scheme to show any special mistrust, I merely smiled a little grimly, and cast a glance at the table on which stood a bottle of brandy and one glass.

" 'Very good brandy,' he whispered, 'Not such stuff as we give those fellows down-stairs.'

" I shrugged my shoulders and he slowly backed towards the door.

" 'The young men you bid me watch are very quiet,' I suggested, with a careless wave of my hand towards the room he had mentioned.

" 'Oh, there is no one there yet. They begin to straggle in about ten o'clock.'

" 'Ah,' was my quiet rejoinder, 'I am likely, then, to have use for your brandy.'

" He smiled again and made a swift motion towards the door.

" 'If you want anything,' said he, 'just step to the foot of the staircase and let me know. The whole establishment is at your service.' And with one final grin that remains in my mind as the most threatening and diabolical I have ever witnessed, he laid his hand on the knob of the door and slid quickly out.

It was done with such an air of final farewell, that I felt my apprehensions take a positive form. Rushing towards the door through which he had just vanished, I listened and heard, as I thought, his stealthy feet descend the stair. But when I sought to follow, I found myself for the second time overwhelmed by darkness. The gas jet, which had hitherto burned with great brightness in the small room, had been turned off from below, and beyond the faint glimmer which found its way through the small window of which I have spoken, not a ray of light now disturbed the heavy gloom of this gruesome apartment.

"I had thought of every contingency but this, and for a few minutes my spirits were dashed. But I soon recovered some remnants of self-possession, and began feeling for the knob I could no longer see. Finding it after a few futile attempts, I was relieved to discover that this door at least was not locked;

and, opening it with a careful hand, I listened intently, but could hear nothing save the smothered sound of men talking in the room below.

"Should I signal for my companions? No, for the secret was not yet mine as to how men passed from this room into the watery grave which was the evident goal for all wearers of the blue ribbon.

"Stepping back into the middle of the room, I carefully pondered my situation, but could get no further than the fact that I was somehow, and in some way, in mortal peril. Would it come in the form of a bullet, or a deadly thrust from an unseen knife? I did not think so. For, to say nothing of the darkness, there was one reassuring fact which recurred constantly to my mind in connection with the murders I was endeavoring to trace to this den of iniquity.

"None of the gentlemen who had been found drowned had shown any marks of violence on their bodies, so it was not attack I was to fear, but some mysterious, underhanded treachery which would rob me of consciousness and make the precipitation of my body into the water both safe and easy. Perhaps it was in the bottle of brandy that the peril lay; perhaps—but why speculate further! I would watch till midnight and then, if nothing happened, signal my companions to raid the house.

"Meantime a peep into the next room might help me towards solving the mystery. Setting the bottle and glass aside, I dragged the table across the floor, placed it under the lighted window, mounted, and was about to peer through, when the light in that apartment was put out also. Angry and overwhelmed, I leapt down, and, stretching out my hands till they touched the wainscoting, I followed the wall around till I came to the knob of the door, which I frantically clutched. But I did not turn it immediately, I was too anxious to catch these villains at work. Would I be conscious of the harm they meditated against me, or would I imperceptibly yield to some influence of which I was not yet conscious, and drop to the floor before I could draw my revolver or put to my mouth the whistle upon which I depended for assistance and safety? It was hard to tell, but I determined to cling to my first intention a little longer, and so stood waiting and counting the minutes, while wondering if the captain of the police boat was not getting impatient, and whether I had not more to fear from the anxiety of my friends than the cupidity of my foes.

"You see I had anticipated communicating with the men in this boat by certain signals and tokens which had been arranged between us. But the lack of windows in the room had made all such arrangements futile, so I knew as little of their actions as they of my sufferings; all of which did not tend to add to the cheerfulness of my position.

"I, however, held out for a half-hour, listening, waiting and watching in a darkness which, like that of Egypt, could be felt, and when the suspense grew intolerable I struck a match and let its blue flame flicker for a moment over the face of my watch. But the matches soon gave out and with them my patience, if not my courage, and I determined to end the suspense by knocking at the door beneath.

"This resolution taken, I pulled open the door before me and stepped out. Though I could see nothing, I remembered the narrow landing at the top of the stairs, and, stretching out my arms, I felt for the boarding on either hand, guilding myself by it, and began to descend, when something rising, as it were, out of the cavernous darkness before me made me halt and draw back in mingled dread and horror.

"But the impression, strong as it was, was only momentary, and, resolved to be done with the matter, I precipitated myself downward, when suddenly, at about the middle of the staircase, my feet slipped and I slid forward, plunging and reaching out with hands whose frenzied grasp found nothing to cling to, down a steep inclined plane—or what to my bewildered senses appeared such,—till I struck a yielding surface and passed with one sickening plunge into the icy waters of the river which in another moment had closed dark and benumbing above my head.

"It was all so rapid I did not think of uttering a cry. But happily for me the splash I made told the story, and I was rescued before I could sink a second time.

"It was a full half hour before I had sufficiently recovered from the shock to relate my story. But when once I had made it known, you can imagine the gusto with which the police prepared to enter the house and confound the obliging host with a sight of my dripping garments and accusing face. And indeed in all my professional experience I have never beheld a more sudden merging of the bully into a coward than was to be seen in this slick villain's face, when I was suddenly pulled from the crowd and placed before him, with the old man's wig gone from my head, and the tag of blue ribbon still clinging to my wet coat.

" His game was up, and he saw it ; and Ebenezer Gryce's career had begun.

" Like all destructive things the device by which I had been run into the river was simple enough when understood. In the first place it had been constructed to serve the purpose of a stairway and chute. The latter was in plain sight when it was used by the sailmakers to run the finished sails into the waiting yawls below. At the time of my adventure, and for some time before, the possibilities of the place had been discovered by mine host, who had ingeniously put a partition up the entire stairway, dividing the steps from the smooth runway. At the upper part of the runway he had built a few steps, wherewith to lure the unwary far enough down to insure a fatal descent. To make sure of his game he had likewise ceiled the upper room all around, including the enclosure of the stairs. The door to the chute and the door to the stairs were side by side, and being made of the same boards as the wainscoting, were scarcely visible when closed, while the single knob that was used, being transferable from one to the other, naturally gave the impression that there was but one door. When this adroit villain called my attention to the little window around the corner, he no doubt removed the knob from the stairs' door and quickly placed it in the one opening upon the chute. Another door, connecting the two similar landings without, explains how he got from the chute staircase into which he passed, on leaving me, to the one communicating with the room below.

"The mystery was solved, and my footing on the force secured ; but to this day—and I am an old man now—I have not forgotten the horror of the moment when my feet slipped from under me, and I felt myself sliding downward, without hope of rescue, into a pit of heaving waters, where so many men of conspicuous virtue had already ended their valuable lives.

"Myriad thoughts flashed through my brain in that brief interval, and among them the whole method of operating this death-trap, together with every detail of evidence that would secure the conviction of the entire gang."

THE HERMIT OF —— STREET

THE HERMIT OF —— STREET.[1]

CHAPTER I.

I COMMIT AN INDISCRETION.

I SHOULD have kept my eyes for the many brilliant and interesting sights constantly offered me. Another girl would have done so. I myself might have done so, had I been over eighteen, or, had I not come from the country, where my natural love of romance had been fostered by uncongenial surroundings and a repressed life under the eyes of a severe and unsympathetic maiden aunt.

I was visiting in a house where fashionable people made life a perpetual holiday. Yet of all the pleasures which followed so rapidly, one upon another, that I have difficulty now in separating them into distinct impressions, the greatest, the only one I never confounded with any other, was the hour I spent in my window after the day's dissipations were all over, watching—what? Truth and the necessities of my story oblige me to say—a man's face, a man's handsome but preoccupied face, bending night after night over a study-table in the lower room of the great house in our rear.

I had been in the city three weeks, and I had already received—pardon the seeming egotism of the confession—four offers, which, considering I had no fortune and but little education or knowledge of the great world, speaks well for something: I leave you to judge what. All of these offers were from young men; one of them from a very desirable young man, but I had listened to no one's addresses, because, after accepting them, I should have felt it wrong to contemplate so unremittingly the face, which, for all its unconsciousness of myself, held me spell-bound to an idea I neither stopped nor cared to analyze.

Why, at such a distance and under circumstances of such distraction, did it affect me so? It was not a young face (Mr. Allison at that time was thirty-five); neither was it a cheerful or even a satisfied one; but it was very handsome, as I have said; far too handsome, indeed, for a romantic girl to see unmoved, and it was an enigmatic face; one that did not lend itself to immediate comprehension, and that, to one of my temperament, was a fatal attraction, especially as enough was known of his more than peculiar habits to assure me that character, rather than whim, lay back of his eccentricities.

But first let me explain more fully my exact position in regard to this gentleman on that day in early spring, destined to be such a memorable one in my history.

I had never seen him, save in the surreptitious way I have related, and he had never seen me. The day following my arrival in the city I had noticed the large house in our rear, and had asked some questions about it. This was but natural, for it was one of the few mansions in the great city with an old-style lawn about it. Besides, it had a peculiarly secluded and secretive look, which even to my unaccustomed eyes, gave it an appearance strangely out of keeping with the expensive but otherwise ordinary houses visible in all other directions. The windows—and there were many—were all shuttered and closed, with the exception of the three on the lower floor and two others directly over these. On the top story they were even boarded up, giving to that portion of the house a blank and desolate air, matched, I was told, by that of the large drawing-room windows on either side of the front door, which faced, as you must see, on another street.

The grounds which, were more or less carefully looked after, were separated from the street by a brick wall, surmounted by urns, from which drooped the leafless tendrils of some old vines ; but in the rear, that is, in our direction, the line of separation was marked by a high iron fence, in which, to my surprise, I saw a gate, which, though padlocked now, marked old habits of intercourse, interesting to contemplate, between the two houses. Through this fence I caught glimpses of the green turf and scattered shrubs of a yard which had once sloped away to the avenues on either side, and, more interesting still, those three windows whose high-drawn shades offered such a vivid contrast to the rest of the house.

In one of these windows stood a table, with a chair before it. I had as yet seen no one in the chair, but I had noted that the table was heavily covered with papers and books, and judged that the room was a library and the table that of a busy man engaged in an endless amount of study and writing.

The Vandykes, whom I had questioned on the matter, were very short in their replies. Not because the subject was uninteresting, or one they in any way sought to avoid, but because the invitations to a great party had just come in, and no other topic was worthy their discussion. But I learned this much. That the house belonged to one of New York's oldest families. That its present owner was a widow of great eccentricity of character, who, with her one child, a daughter, unfortunately blind from birth, had taken up her abode in some foreign country, where she thought her child's affliction would attract less attention than in her native city. The house had been closed to the extent I have mentioned, immediately upon her departure, but had not been left entirely empty. Mr. Allison, her man of business, had moved into it, and, being fully as eccentric as herself, had contented himself for five years with a solitary life in this dismal mansion, without friends, almost without acquaintances, though he might have had unlimited society and any amount of attention, his personal attractions being of a very uncommon order, and his talent for business so pronounced, that he was already recognized at thirty-five as one of the men to be afraid of in Wall Street. Of his birth and connections little was known; he was called the Hermit of —— Street, and—well, that is about all they told me at this time.

After I came to see him (as I did that very evening), I could ask no further questions concerning him. The beauty of his countenance, the mystery of his secluded life, the air of melancholy and mental distress which I imagined myself to detect in his manner—he often used to sit for minutes together with his eyes fixed on vacancy and his whole face expressive of the bitterest emotion—had wrought this spell upon my imagination, and I could no more mingle his name with that of the ordinary men and women we discussed than I could confound his solitary and expressive figure with the very proper but conventional forms of the simpering youths who followed me in parlors or begged to be allowed the honor of a dance at the balls I attended with the Vandykes. He occupied an unique place in my regard, and this without another human being's knowledge. I wish I could say without my own; but, alas! I have promised myself to be true in all the details of this history, and, child as I was, I could not be ignorant of the fascination which held me for hours at my window when I should have been in bed and asleep.

But let me hasten to the adventure which put an end to my dreams by launching me into realities of a still more absorbing nature. I was not very well one day, and even Mrs. Vandyke acknowledged that it would not do for me to take the long-planned drive to Tuxedo. So, as I would not let any one else miss this pleasure on my account, I had been left alone in the house, and, not being ill enough for bed, had spent the most of the morning in my window—not because he was in his; I was yet too timid, and, let me hope, too girlishly modest, to wish to attract in any way his attention--but because the sun shone there, and I was just chilly enough to enjoy its mingled light and heat. Thus it was I came to notice the following petty occurrence. In the yard of the house next to that occupied by Mr. Allison was kept a tame rabbit, which often took advantage of a hole it had made for itself under the dividing fence to roam over the neighboring lawn. On this day he was taking his accustomed ramble, when something startled him, and he ran, not back to his hole, but to our fence, through which he squeezed himself, evidently to his own great discomfort; for once in our yard, and under the refuge of a small bush he found there, nothing would lure him back, though every effort was made to do so, both by the small boy to whom he belonged, and the old serving-man or gardener, who was the only other person besides Mr. Allison whom I ever saw on the great place. Watching them, I noted three things: first, that it was the child who first thought of opening the gate; secondly, that it was the serving-man who brought the key; and, thirdly, that after the gate had been opened and the rabbit recovered, the gate had not been locked again; for, just as the man was about to do this, a call came from the front, of so imperative a nature, that he ran forward, without readjusting the padlock, and did not come back, though I watched for him in idle curiosity for a good half-hour. This was in the morning. At seven o'clock—how well I remember the hour!—I was sitting again in my window, waiting for the return of the Vandykes, and watching the face which had now reappeared at its usual place in the study. It was dark everywhere save there, and I was marveling over the sense of companionship it gave me under circumstances of loneliness, which some girls might have felt most keenly, when suddenly my attention was drawn from him to a window in the story over his head, by the rapid blowing in and out of a curtain, which had been left hanging loose before an open sash. As there was a lighted gas-jet near by, I watched the gyrating muslin with some apprehension, and was more shocked than astonished when, in another moment, I saw the flimsy folds give one wild flap and flare up into a brilliant and dangerous flame. To shriek and throw up my window was the work of a moment, but I attracted no attention by these means, and, what was worse, saw, with feelings which may be imagined, that nothing I could do would be likely to arouse Mr. Allison to an immediate sense of his danger, for not only were the windows shut between us, but he was lost in one of his brooding spells, which to all appearance made him quite impassible to surrounding events.

"Will no one see? Will no one warn him?" I cried out, in terror of the flames burning so brightly in the room above him. Seemingly not. No other window was raised in the vicinity, and, frightened quite beyond the exercise of reason or any instincts of false modesty, I dashed out of my room downstairs, calling for the servants. But Lucy was in the front area and Ellen above, and I was on the back porch and in the garden before either of them responded.

Meanwhile, no movement was observable in the brooding figure of Mr. Allison, and no diminution in the red glare which now filled the room above him. To see him sitting there so much at his ease, and to behold at the same moment the destruction going on so rapidly over his head, affected me more than I can tell, and casting to the winds all selfish considerations, I sprang through the gate so providentially left ajar and knocked with all my might on a door which opened upon a side porch not many feet away from the spot where he sat so unconcernedly.

The moment I had done this I felt like running away again, but hearing his advancing step, summoned up my courage and stood my ground bravely, determined to say one word and run.

But when the door opened and I found myself face to face with the man whose face I knew only too well, that word, important as it was, stuck in my throat; for, agitated as I was, both by my errand and my sudden encounter with one I had dreamed about for weeks, he seemed to be much more so, though by other reasons—by far other reasons—than myself. He was so moved—was it by the appearance of a strange young girl on his doorstep, or was it at something in my face or manner, or something in his thoughts to which that face or manner gave a shock?—that my petty fears for the havoc going on above seemed to pale into insignificance before the emotions called up by my presence. Confronting me with dilating eyes, he faltered slowly back till his natural instincts of courtesy recalled him to himself, and he bowed, when I found courage to cry:

"Fire! Your house is on fire! Up there, overhead!"

The sound which left his lips as these words slipped from mine struck me speechless again. Appalling as the cry "Fire!" is at all times and to all men, it roused in this man at this time something beyond anything my girlish soul had ever imagined of terror or dismay. So intense were the feelings I saw aroused in him that I expected to see him rush into the open air with loud cries for help. But instead of that, he pushed the door to behind me, and locking me in, said, in a strange and hoarsened tone:

"Don't call out, don't make any sound or outcry, and above all, don't let any one in; I will fight the flames alone!" and seizing a lamp from the study-table, he dashed from me towards a staircase I could faintly see in the distance. But half-way down the hall he looked back at me, and again I saw that look on his face which had greeted my unexpected appearance in the doorway.

Alas! it was a thrilling look—a look which no girl could sustain without emotion; and spell-bound under it, I stood in a maze, alone and in utter darkness, not knowing whether to unlock the door and escape or to stand still and wait for his reappearance, as he evidently expected me to do.

Meanwhile, the alarm had spread, and more than one cry arose from the houses in the rear. I could hear feet running over the walks without, and finally a knock on the door I was leaning against, followed by the cry:

"Let us in! Fire! fire!"

But I neither moved nor answered. I was

afraid to be found there, crouching alone in a bachelor's residence, but I was equally afraid of disobeying him, for his voice had been very imperious when he commanded me not to let any one in; and I was too young to brave such a nature, even if I had wished to, which I do not think I did.

"He is overhead! See him—see him!" I now heard shouted from the lawn. "He has dragged the curtains down! He is showering the walls with water! Look—look! how wildly he works! He will be burnt himself. Ah! ah!" All of which gave me strange thrills, and filled the darkness which encompassed me with startling pictures, till I could hardly stand the stress or keep myself from rushing to his assistance.

While my emotions were at their height a bell rang. It was the front doorbell, and it meant the arrival of the engines.

"Oh!" thought I, "what shall I do now? If I run out I shall encounter half the neighborhood in the back yard; if I stay here how shall

I be able to meet the faces of the firemen who will come rushing in?"

But I was not destined to suffer from either contingency. As the bell rang a second time, a light broke on the staircase I was so painfully watching, and Mr. Allison descended, lamp in hand, as he had gone up. He appeared calm now, and without any show of emotion proceeded at once to the front door, which he opened.

What passed between him and the policeman whose voice I heard in the hall, I do not know. I heard them go up-stairs and presently come down again, and I finally heard the front door close. Then I began to make an effort to gain some control over my emotions, for I knew he had not forgotten me, and that he soon would be in the vestibule at my side.

But it was impossible for me to hope to meet him with an unconcerned air. The excitement I was under and the cold—for I was dressed lightly and the vestibule was chilly—had kept me trembling so; that my curls had fallen all about my cheeks, and one had fallen so low that it hung in shameful disorder to my very waist. This alone was enough to disconcert me, but had my heart been without its secret—a secret I was in mortal terror of disclosing in my confusion—I could have risen above my embarrassment and let simple haste been my excuse. As it was, I must have met him with a pleading aspect, very much like that of a frightened child, for his countenance visibly changed as he approached me, and showed quite an extraordinary kindness, if not contrition, as he paused in the narrow vestibule with the blazing lamp held low in his hand.

"My little girl," he began, but instantly changed the phrase to "My dear young lady, how can I thank you enough, and how can I sufficiently express my regret at having kept you a prisoner in this blazing house? I fear I have frightened you sorely, but——" And here, to my astonishment, he found nothing to say, moved overmuch by some strong feeling, or checked in his apologies by some great embarrassment.

Astonished, for he did not look like a man who could be lightly disturbed, I glowed a fiery red and put my hand out towards the door. Instantly he found speech again.

"One moment," said he. "I feel that I ought to explain the surprise, the consternation, which made me forget. You know this is not my house, that I am here in trust for another, that the place is full of rare treasures."

Had he stopped again? I was in such a state of inner perturbation that I hardly knew whether he had ceased to speak or I to hear. Something, I did not know what, had shaken my very life's center—something in the shape of dread, yet so mixed with delight that my hand fell from the knob I had been blindly groping for and sank heavily at my side. His eyes had not left my face.

"May I ask whom I have the honor of addressing?" he asked, in a tone I might better never have heard from his lips.

To this I must make reply. Shuddering, for I felt something uncanny in the situation, but speaking up, notwithstanding, with the round and vibrating tones I had inherited from my mother, I answered, with the necessary simplicity:

"I am Delight Hunter, a country girl, sir, visiting the Vandykes."

A flash that was certainly one of pleasure lighted up his face with a brilliance fatal to my poor, quivering girl's heart.

"Allow me, Miss Hunter, to believe that you will not bring down the indignation of my neighbors upon me by telling them of my carelessness and indiscretion." Then, as my lips settled into a determined curve, he himself opened the door, and bowing low, asked if I would accept his protection to the gate.

But at the rush of the night air, such a sensation of shame overpowered me that I only thought of retreat; and, declining his offer with a wild shake of the head, I dashed from the house and fled with an incomprehensible sense of relief back to that of the Vandykes. The servants, who had seen me rush towards Mr. Allison's, were still in the yard watching for me. I did not vouchsafe them a word. I could hardly formulate words in my own mind. A great love and a great dread had seized upon me at once. A great love for the man by whose face I had been moved for weeks and a great dread--well, I cannot explain my dread, not as I felt it that night. It was formless and without apparent foundation ; but it would no more leave me than my uneasy memory of the fierce instinct which had led him at such a critical instant to close his door against all help, though in so doing he had subjected a young girl to many minutes of intense embarrassment and mortifying indecision.

CHAPTER II.

A STRANGE WEDDING BREAKFAST.

Mr. Allison, who had never before been known to leave his books and papers, not only called the next day to express his gratitude for what he was pleased to style my invaluable warning, but came every day after, till not only my heart but my reason told me that the great house in the rear might ultimately be my home, if the passion which had now become my life should prove greater than the dread which had not yet entirely left me.

Mr. Allison loved me—oh, what pride in the thought!—but Mr. Allison had a secret, or why did he so often break off abruptly in some telltale speech and drop his eyes, which were otherwise always upon me. Something not easy to understand lay between us—something which he alternately defied and succumbed to, something which kept him from being quite the good man I had pictured myself as marrying. Why I was so certain of this latter fact, I cannot say. Perhaps my instinct was keen; perhaps the signs of goodness are so unmistakable that even a child feels their want where her heart leans hardest.

Yet everything I heard of him only tended to raise him in my estimation. After he became an habitué of the house, Mrs. Vandyke grew more communicative in regard to him. He was eccentric, of course, but his eccentricities were such as did him credit. One thing she told me made a lasting impression on me. Mrs. Ransome, the lady in whose house he lived, had left her home very suddenly. He anticipated a like return; so, ever since her departure, it had been his invariable custom to have the table set for three, so that he might never be surprised by her arrival. It had become a monomania with him. Never did he sit down without there being enough before him for a small family, and as his food was all brought in cooked from a neighboring restaurant, this eccentricity of his was well known, and gave an added *éclat* to his otherwise hermit-like habits. To my mind, it added an element of pathos to his seclusion, and so affected me that one day I dared to remark to him :

"You must have liked Mrs. Ransome very much you are so faithful in your remembrance of her."

I never presumed again to attack any of his foibles. He gave me first a hard look, then an indulgent one, and finally managed to say, after a moment of quiet hesitation :

"You allude to my custom of setting two chairs at the table to which they may return at any minute? Miss Hunter, what I do in the loneliness of that great house is not worth the gossip of those who surround you."

Flushing till I wished my curls would fall down and hide my cheeks, I tried to stammer out some apology. But he drove it back with a passionate word :

"Delight, idol of my heart, come and see

what a lonely place that old house is. Come and live in that house—at least for a little time, till I can arrange for you a brighter and a happier home—come and be my wife."

It was sudden, it was all but unlooked-for, and like all his expressions of feeling, frenzied rather than resolute. But it was a declaration that met my most passionate longings, and in the elation it brought I forgot for the moment the doubts it called up. Otherwise I had been a woman rather than a girl, and this tale had never been written.

"You love me, Delight" (he was already pressing me in his arms), "you love me or you would never have rushed so impetuously to warn me of my danger that night. Make me the maddest, happiest man in all the world by saying you will not wait; that you will not ask counsel of anybody or anything but your affection, but marry me at once; marry me while my heart yearns for you so deeply; marry me before I go away——"

"Go away?"

"Yes, I am going away. Mrs. Ransome and her daughter are coming back and I am going away. Will you go with me?"

With what intensity he spoke, yet with what hardness. I quivered while I listened, yet I made no move to withdraw from him. Had he asked me to step with him from the house-top I should hardly have refused while his heart throbbed so wildly against mine and his eyes lured me on with such a promise of ecstasy.

"You will?" How peremptory he could be. "You will?" How triumphant, also.

I hardly realized what I had done till I stood abashed before Mrs. Vandyke, and told her I had engaged myself to marry Mr. Allison before he went to Europe. Then it seemed I had done a very good thing. She congratulated me heartily, and, seeing I had a certain fear of taking my aunt into my confidence, promised to sit down and write to her herself, using every encomium she could think of to make this sudden marriage, on my part, seem like the result of reason and wise forethought.

" Such an estimable man! such an old neighbor! so domestic in his tastes! and, oh! so wise to find out and make his own the slyest and most bewildering little beauty that has come into New York this many a season!" These were some of her words, and, though pleasing at the time, they made me think deeply—much more deeply than I wished to, after I went upstairs to my room.

" Estimable! an old neighbor! domestic in his tastes!" Had she said: " Handsome! masterful in his air and spirit! a man to make a girl forget the real end of life and think only of present pleasure!" I should not have had such a fierce reaction. But estimable! Was he estimable? I tried to cry out yes! I tried to keep down the memory of that moment when, with a dozen passions suddenly let loose (one of them fear), he strode by me and locked the door against all help, under an impetus he had tried in vain to explain. Nothing would quiet the still, small voice speaking in my breast, or give to the moment that unalloyed joy which belongs to a young girl's betrothal. I was afraid. Why?

Mr. Allison never came in the evening, another of his peculiarities. Other men did, but what were other men to me now? This night I pleaded weariness (Mrs. Vandyke understood me), and remained in my room. I wanted to study the face of my lover under the new conditions. Was he in his old seat? Yes. And would he read, as usual, or study? No. He had thoughts of his own to-night, engrossing enough to hold him enthralled without the aid of his ordinary occupations; thoughts, thoughts of me, thoughts which should have cleared his brow and made his face a study of delight to me. But was it so? Alas! I had never seen it so troubled; lit with gleams of hope or happiness by spells, but mostly sunk in depths of profoundest contemplation, which gave to it a melancholy from which I shrank, and not the melancholy one longs to comfort and allay. What was on his mind? What was in his heart? Something he feared to have noted, for suddenly he rose with a start, and, for the first time since my eyes had sought that window, pulled down the shades and thus shut himself out from my view altogether. Was it a rebuke to my insistent watchfulness? or the confession of a reticent nature fearing to be surprised in its moment of weakness? I ought to know—I would know. To-morrow I would ask him if there was any sorrow in his life which a confiding girl ought to be made acquainted with before she yielded him her freedom. But the pang which pierced me at the thought, proved that I feared his answer too much to ever question him.

I am thus explicit in regard to my thoughts and feelings at this time, that I may more fully account to you for what I did later. I had not, what every one else seemed to have, full confidence in this man, and yet the thrall in which I was held by the dominating power of his passion, kept me from seeking that advice even from my own intuitions, which might have led to my preservation. I was blind and knew I was blind, yet rushed on headlong. I asked him no questions till our wedding day.

My aunt, who seemed quite satisfied with Mrs. Vandyke's explanations, promised to be present at the ceremony, which was set at an alarmingly near day. My lovers on the contrary—by whom I mean the half dozen men who had been attentive to me—refused to attend, so I had one care less; for the lack of time—perhaps I should say my lack of means—precluded me from obtaining a very elaborate wedding dress, and I did not choose to have them see me appear on such an occasion in any less charming guise than I had been accustomed to wear at party or play. *He* did not care what I wore. When I murmured something about the haste with which he had hurried things forward, and how it was likely to interfere with what most brides considered necessary to the proper celebration of such an event, he caught me to his breast with a feverish gesture and vowed that if he could have his way, there would be no preparation at all, but just a ceremony before a minister which would make me his without the least delay.

Men may enjoy such precipitation, but women do not. I was so troubled by what seemed the meagerness of my wardrobe and the lack of everything I had been accustomed to see brides bring their husbands, that I asked Mrs. Vandyke one day if Mr. Allison was a rich man. She answered, with a smile: "No, my dear, not as we New-Yorkers count riches. Having the power of attorney for Mrs. Ransome, he handles a good deal of money; but very little of it is his own, though to you his five-thousand-a-year salary may seem a fortune."

This was so much Greek to me, though I did understand he was not considered wealthy.

"Then my fawn-colored cloth will not be so very inappropriate for a wedding dress?" I asked.

"I wish you could see yourself in it," she said, and that satisfied me.

We were married simply, but to the sound

of wonderful music, in a certain little church not far from —— Street. My aunt was there and my four lovers, though they had said, one and all, they would not come. But I saw nothing, realized nothing, save the feverish anxiety of my bridegroom, who, up to the minute the final vows were uttered, seemed to be on a strain of mingled emotions, among which I seemed to detect that old one of fear. A pitiful outlook for an adoring bride, you will think, who, without real friends to interest themselves in her, allows herself to be pushed to a brink she is wise enough to see, but not strong enough to recoil from. Yes, but its full pathos did not strike me then. I only felt anxious to have the ceremony over, to know that the die was cast beyond my own powers of retraction; and when the words of the benediction at last fell upon my ears, it was with real joy I turned to see if they brought him as much rapture as they did me. Happily for that moment's satisfaction they did, and if a friend had been there with eyes to see and heart to feel, there would have been nothing in the air of open triumph with which Mr. Allison led me down the aisle to awaken aught but hope and confidence. My own hopes rose at the sight, and when at the carriage door he turned to give me a smile before he helped me in, nothing but the obstinacy of my nature prevented me from accepting the verdict of my acquaintances, "That for a little country girl, with nothing but her good looks to recommend her, Delight Hunter had done remarkably well in the one short month she had been in the city."

Mr. Allison had told me that it would be impossible for him to take me out of the city at present. It was therefore to the house on —— Street we were driven. On the way he attempted to reconcile me to what he feared might strike me as dreary in the prospect.

"The house is partially closed," said he, "and many of the rooms are locked. Even the great drawing-rooms have an uninhabited look, which will make them anything but attractive to a lover of sunshine and comfort; but the library is cheerful, and in that you can sit and imagine yourself at home till I can wind up my business affairs and make possible the trip upon which I have set my heart."

"Does that mean," I faintly ventured, "that you will leave me to spend much of my time alone in that great echoing house?"

"No," was his quick response, "you shall spend no time there alone. When I go out you shall go too, and if business takes me where you cannot accompany me I will give you money to shop with, which will keep you pleasantly occupied till I can rejoin you. Oh, we will make it a happy honeymoon, in spite of all obstacles, my darling. I should be a wretch if I did not make it happy for *you*."

Here was my opportunity. I trembled as I thought of it, and stammered quite like a foolish child as I softly suggested:

"For me? Is it not likely to be a happy one for *you?*"

I will not give his answer; it was a passionate one, but it was not convincing. Pondering it and trying to persuade myself he alluded only to business cares and anxieties, I let the minute slip by and entered the house with doubts unsolved, but with no further effort to understand him. Remember, he was thirty-five and I but a chit of eighteen.

In the hall stood the old serving-man with whose appearance I was already so familiar. He had a smile on his face, which formed my only welcome. He also had a napkin over his arm.

"Luncheon is served," he announced, with great formality; and then I saw through an open door the glitter of china and glass, and realized I was about to take my first meal with my husband.

Mr. Allison had already told me that he intended to make no changes in his domestic arrangements for the few days we were likely to occupy this house. I had therefore expected that our meals would be served from the restaurant, and that Ambrose (the waiting-man) would continue to be the only other occupant of the house. But I was not sure whether the table would be still set for four, or whether he would waive this old custom now that he had a wife to keep him company at the once lonely board. I was eager to know, and as soon as I could lay aside my hat in the little reception-room, I turned my face towards the dining-room door, where my husband stood awaiting me with a bunch of great white roses in his hand.

"Sweets to the sweet," said he, with a smile that sunk down deep into my heart and made my eyes moisten with joy. In the hackneyed expression there rang nothing false. He was proud and he was glad to see me enter that dining-room as his wife.

The next moment I was before the board, which had been made as beautiful as possible with flowers and the finest of dinner services. But the table was set for four, two of whom could only be present in spirit.

I wondered if I were glad or sorry to see it

—if I were more pleased with his loyalty to his absent employer, or disappointed that my presence had not made everybody else forgotten. To be consistent, I should have rejoiced at this evidence of sterling worth on his part; but girls are not consistent—at least, brides of an hour are not—and I may have pouted the least bit in the world as I pointed to the two places set as elaborately as our own, and said with the daring which comes with the rights of a wife:

"It would be a startling coincidence if Mrs. Ransome and her daughter should return to-day. I fear I would not like it."

I was looking directly at him as I spoke, with a smile on my lips and my hand on the back of my chair. But the jest I had expected in reply did not come. Something in my tone or choice of topic jarred upon him, and his answer was a simple wave of his hand towards Ambrose, who at once relieved me of my bouquet, placing it in a tall glass at the side of my plate.

"Now we will sit," said he.

I do not know how the meal would have passed had Ambrose not been present. As it was, it was a rather formal affair, and would have been slightly depressing, if I had not caught, now and then, flashing glances from my husband's eye which assured me that he found as much to enchain him in my presence as I did in his. What we ate I have no idea of. I only remember that in every course there was enough for four.

As we rose, I was visited by a daring impulse. Ambrose had poured me out a glass of wine, which stood beside my plate undisturbed. As I stooped to recover my flowers again, I saw this glass, and at once lifted it towards him, crying:

"To Mrs. Ransome and her daughter, who did *not* return to enjoy our wedding-breakfast."

He recoiled. Yes, I am sure he gave a start back, though he recovered himself immediately and responded with grave formality to my toast.

"Does he not like Mrs. Ransome?" I thought. "Is the somewhat onerous custom he maintains here the result of a sense of duty rather than of liking?"

My curiosity was secretly whetted by the thought. But with a girl's lightness I began to talk of other things, and first of the house, which I now for the first time looked at with anything like seeing eyes.

He was patient with me, but I perceived he did not enjoy this topic any more than the former one. "It is not ours," he kept saying; "remember that none of these old splendors are ours."

"They are more ours than they are Mrs. Ransome's, just now," I at last retorted, with one of my girlhood's saucy looks. "At all events, I am going to play that it is ours tonight," I added, dancing away from him towards the long drawing-rooms where I hoped to come upon a picture of the absent lady of the house.

"Delight"—he was quite peremptory now—

"I must ask you not to enter those rooms, however invitingly the doors may stand open. It is a notion, a whim of mine, that you do not lend your beauty to light up that ghostly collection of old pictures and ugly upholstery, and if you feel like respecting my wishes——"

"But may I not stand in the doorway?" I asked, satisfied at having been able to catch a glimpse of a full-length portrait of a lady who could be no other than Mrs. Ransome. "See! my shadow does not even fall across the carpet. I won't do the room any harm, and I am sure that Mrs. Ransome's picture won't do me any."

"Come! come away!" he cried; and humoring his wishes, I darted away, this time in the direction of the dining-room and Ambrose. "My dear," remonstrated my husband, quickly following me, "what has brought you back here?"

"I want to see," said I, "what Ambrose does with the food we did not eat. Such a lot of it!"

It was childish, but then I was a child and a nervous one, too. Perhaps he considered this, for, while he was angry enough to turn pale, he did not attempt any rebuke, but left it to Ambrose to say:

"Mr. Allison is very good, ma'am. This food, which is very nice, is given each day to a poor girl who comes for it, and takes it home to her parents. I put it in this basket, and Mr. Allison gives it to the girl when she calls for it in the evening."

"You *are* good," I cried, turning to my husband with a fond look. Did he think the emphasis misplaced, or did he consider it time for me to begin to put on more womanly ways, for drawing me again into the library, he made me sit beside him on the big lounge, and after a kiss or two, demanded quietly, but oh, how peremptorily:

"Delight, why do you so often speak of Mrs. Ransome? Have you any reason for it? Has any one talked to you about her, that her name seems to be almost the only one on your lips in the few, short minutes we have been married?"

I did not know why this was so, myself, so I only shook my head and sighed, repentingly. Then, seeing that he would have some reply, I answered with what *naiveté* I could summon up at the moment:

"I think it was because you seem so ashamed of your devotion to them. I love to see your embarrassment, founded as it is upon the most generous instincts."

His hand closed over mine with a fierceness that hurt me.

"Let us talk of love," he whispered. "Delight, this is our wedding-day."

CHAPTER III.

ONE BEAD FROM A NECKLACE.

AFTER supper Mr. Allison put before me a large book. "Amuse yourself with these pictures," said he; "I have a little task to perform. After it is done I will come again and sit with you."

"You are not going out," I cried, starting up.

"No," he smiled, "I am not going out."

I sank back and opened the book, but I did not look at the pictures. Instead of that I listened to his steps moving about the house, rear and front, and finally going up what seemed to be a servant's staircase, for I could see the great front stairs from where I sat, and there was no one on them. "Why do I not hear his feet overhead?" I asked myself. "That is the only room he has given me leave to enter. Does his task take him elsewhere?" Seemingly so, for, though he was gone a good half hour, he did not enter the room above. Why should I think of so small a matter? It would be hard to say; perhaps I was afraid of being left in the great rooms alone; perhaps I was only curious; but I asked myself a dozen times before he reappeared, "Where is he gone, and why does he stay away so long?" But when he returned and sat down I said nothing. There was a little thing I noted, however. His hands were trembling, and it was five minutes before he met my inquiring look. This I should not consider worth mentioning if I had not observed the same hesitancy follow the same disappearance up-stairs on the succeeding night. It was the only time in the day when he really left me, and, when he came back, he was not like himself for a good half hour or more. "I will not displease him with questions," I decided; "but some day I will find my own way into those lofts above. I shall never be at rest till I do."

What I expected to find there is as much a mystery to my understanding as my other doubts and fears. I hardly think I expected to find anything but a desk of papers, or a box with money in it or other valuables. Still the idea that something on the floor above had power to shadow my husband's face, even in the glow of his first love for me, possessed me so completely that, when he fell asleep one evening on the library lounge, I took the opportunity of stealing away and mounting the forbidden staircase to the third floor. I had found a candle in my bedroom, and this I took to light me. But it revealed nothing to me except a double row of unused rooms, with dust on the handles of all the doors. I scrutinized them all; for, young as I was, I had wit enough to see that if I could find one knob on which no dust lay that would be the one my husband was accustomed to turn. But every one showed tokens of not having been touched in years, and, baffled in my search, I was about to retreat, when I remembered that the house had four stories, and that I had not yet come upon the staircase leading to the one above. A hurried search (for I was mortally afraid of being surprised by my husband,) revealed to me at last a distant door, which had no dust on its knob. It lay at the bottom of a shut-in stair-case, and, convinced that here was the place my husband was in the habit of visiting, I carefully fingered the knob, which turned very softly in my hand. But it did not open the door. There was a lock visible just below, and that lock was fastened.

My first escapade was without visible results, but I was uneasy from that hour. I imagined all sorts of things hidden beyond that closed, door. I remembered that the windows of the fourth story were all boarded up, and asked myself why this had been done when the lower ones had been left open. I was young, but I had heard of occupations which could only be entered into by a man secretly. Did he amuse himself with forbidden tasks in that secluded place above, or was I but exaggerating facts which might have their basis simply in a quondam bachelor's desire for solitude and a quiet smoke. "I will follow him up some night," thought I, "and see if I cannot put an end at once to my unworthy fears and unhappy suspicions." But I never did; something happened very soon to prevent me.

I was walking one morning in the grounds that lay about the house, when suddenly I felt something small but perceptibly hard strike my hat and bound quickly off. Astonished, for I was under no tree, under nothing indeed but the blue of heaven, I looked about for the object that had struck me. As I did so, I perceived my husband in his window, but his eyes, while upon me, did not see me, for no change passed over him as I groped about in the grass. "In one of his contemplative moods," thought I, continuing my search. In another instant I started up. I had found a little thing like a bullet wrapped up in paper; but it was no bullet; it was a bead, a large gold bead, and on the paper which surrounded it were written words so fine I could not at first decipher them, but as soon as I had stepped away far enough to be out of the reach of the eyes I both loved and feared more than any in the world, I managed, by dint of great patience, and by placing the almost transparent paper on which they were written over one of the white satin strings of the cape I wore, to read these words:

"Help from the passing stranger! I am

Elizabeth Ransome, owner of the house in which I have been imprisoned five years. Search for me in the upper story. You will find me there with my blind daughter. He who placed us here is below; beware his cunning."

And underneath, these words:

"This is the twenty-fifth attempt I have made to attract attention to our unhappy fate. I can make but two more. There are but two beads left of Theresa's necklace."

"What is the matter, ma'am? Are you ill?" It was Ambrose; I knew his voice.

Crushing the paper in my hand, I tried to look up; but it was in vain. The sting of sudden and complete disillusion had struck me to the heart; I knew my husband to be a villain.

CHAPTER IV.

I LEARN HYPOCRISY.

ONLY eighteen, but from that moment, a woman. Sunk in horror as I was, I yet had wit enough to clap my hands to my head and say I had been dazzled by the sun.

Ambrose, who, in the week I had been with them, had shown himself delighted with the change my coming had made in the house, looked alarmed at this and wanted to call Mr. Allison; but I forbade him, and said I would go in by myself, which I did under a stress of will-power rarely exercised, I dare believe, by a girl so young and so miserable.

"What shall I say to him? how shall I meet him? how can I hide my knowledge and act as if this thing had never been?" For even in that rush of confusing emotions I recognized one fact; that I must not betray by look or word that I knew his dreadful secret. If he were villain enough to keep a woman, and that woman the rightful owner of the property he was himself enjoying, in a prison he had made for her in her own house, then he was villain enough to strangle the one who had discovered this fact, were she the cherished darling of his seared and calculating heart. I was afraid of him now that I knew him, yet I never thought of flying his presence or revealing his crime. He was, villain or no villain, my husband, and nothing could ever undo that fact or make it true that I had never loved him.

So I went in, but went in slowly and with downcast eyes. The bead and the paper I had dropped into my *vinaigrette*, which fortunately hung at my side.

" Humphrey," I said, " when are we going to leave this house? I begin to find it lonesome."

He was preparing to gather up his papers for his accustomed trip down town, but he stopped as I spoke, and look at me curiously.

"You are pale," he remarked, "change and travel will benefit you. Dearest, we will try to sail for Europe in a week."

A week! What did he mean? Leave his prisoners—alas, I understood his journeys to the top of the house now—and go away to Europe? I felt myself grow livid at the thought, and caught a spray of lilac from the table where I stood and held it to my face.

"Will your business affairs warrant it?" I asked. "Are you sure Mrs. Ransome's affairs will not suffer by your absence?" Then, as I saw him turn white, I made a ghastly effort, happily hid by the flowers I held pressed against my face, and suggested, laughingly, "How, if she should come back after your departure! would she meet the greeting she deserves?"

He was half the room away from me, but I heard the click of subdued passion in his throat, and turned sick almost to the point of fainting. "It is four days since you mentioned Mrs. Ransome's name," he said. "When we are gone from here you must promise that it shall never again pass your lips. Mrs. Ransome is not a good woman, Delight."

It was a lie yet his manner of speaking it, and the look with which he now approached me, made me feel helpless again, and I made haste to rush from the room, ostensibly to prepare for our trip down town, in order to escape my own weakness and gain a momentary self-possession before we faced the outside world. Only eighteen years old and confronted by such a diabolical problem!

CHAPTER V.

THE STOLEN KEY.

I WAS too young to reason in those days. Had I not been, had I been able to say to myself that no act requiring such continued precaution could take place in the heart of a great city without ultimate, if not instant, detection, instinct would still have assured me that what

I read was true, however improbable or unheard of it might seem. That the recognition of this fact imposed upon me two almost irreconcilable duties I was slower to perceive. But soon, too soon, it became apparent even to my girlish mind, that, as the wife of the man who had committed this great and inconceivable wrong, I was bound, not only to make an immediate attempt to release the women he so outrageously held imprisoned in their own house, but to so release them that he should escape the opprobrium of his own act.

That I might have time to think, and that I might be saved, if but for one day, contact with one it was almost my duty to hate, I came back to him with the plea that I might spend the day with the Vandykes instead of accompanying him down town as usual. I think he was glad of the freedom my absence offered him, for he gave me the permission I asked, and in ten minutes I was in my old home. Mrs. Vandyke received me with effusion. It was not the first time she had seen me since my marriage, but it was the first time she had seen me alone.

"My dear!" she exclaimed, turning me about till my unwilling face met the light, "is this the wild-wood lassie I gave into Mr. Allison's keeping a week ago!"

"It is the house!" I excitedly gasped, "the empty, lonely, echoing house! I am afraid in it, even with my husband. It gives me creepy feelings, *as if a murder had been committed in it.*"

She broke into a laugh; I hear the sound now, an honest, amused and entirely reassuring laugh, that relieved me in one way and depressed me in another. "The idea! *that* house!" she cried. "I never thought you a girl to have nervous fancies. Why, it is the most matter-of-fact old mansion in the city. All its traditions are of the most respectable kind; no skeleton in those closets! By the way, my dear, has Mr. Allison shown you any of the curious old things those rooms must contain?"

I managed to stammer out a reply, "Mr.

Allison does not consider that his rights extend so far. I have never crossed the drawing-room floor."

"Well! that is carrying honor to an extreme. I am afraid I should not be able to suppress my curiosity to that extent. Is he afraid of the old lady returning unexpectedly and catching him?"

I could not echo her laugh; I could not even smile; I could only pucker up my brows as if angry.

"Everything is kept in shape, so that if she does return she will find the house comfortable," I said; then, with a rising sense of having by this speech suggested a falsehood, I hastily dropped the topic, and, with an entire change of manner, remarked, airily:

"Mrs. Ransome must have gone off very suddenly, to leave everything so exposed in a house as splendid as that. Most people, however rich, see to their choice things more carefully."

She rose to the bait. "Mrs. Ransome is a

queer woman. Her things are of but little account to her; to save her daughter from a moment's pain she would part with the house itself, let alone the accumulations it contains. That is why she left the country so suddenly."

I waited a moment under the pretense of admiring a locket she wore, then I suggested, quietly:

"My husband told you that?"

The answer was as careless as the speaker.

"Oh, I don't know who told me. It's five years ago now, but every one at the time understood that she was angry, because some one mentioned blindness before her daughter. Mrs. Ransome had regarded it as a religious duty to raise her daughter in ignorance of her affliction. When she found she could not do so among her friends and acquaintances, she took her away to a strange land. It is the only tradition, which is not commonplace, which belongs to the family. Let us go up and see my new gowns. I have had two come home from Arnold's since you went away."

I thought the gowns would keep a minute longer. "Did Mrs. Ransome say good-by to her friends?" I asked. "Somehow this matter strikes me as being very romantic."

"Oh, that shows what a puss you are. No, Mrs. Ransome did not say good-by to her friends, that is, not to us. She just went, leaving everything in your husband's charge, who certainly has acquitted himself of the obligation most religiously. And now will you see the gowns?"

I tortured myself by submitting to this ordeal, then I ventured on another and entirely different attempt to clear up the mystery that was fast stifling out my youth, love and hope. I professed to have an extraordinary desire to see the city from the house-top. I had never been any higher up than the third story of any house I had been in, and could not, I told her, go any higher in the house in which I was then living. Might I go up on her roof? Her eyes opened, but she was of an amiable, inconsequent disposition and let me have my way without too much opposition. So, together with a maid she insisted upon sending with me, I made my way through the skylight on to the roof, and so into full view of the neighboring house-tops.

One glance at the spot I was most interested in, and I found myself too dizzy to look further. In the center of Mrs. Ransome's roof there was to be seen what I can best describe as an extended cupola without windows. As there was no other break visible in the roof, the top of this must have held the skylight, which, being thus lifted many feet above the level of the garret floor, would admit air and light enough to the boarded-up space below, but would make any effort to be heard or seen, on the part of any one secreted there, quite ineffectual. One might, by a great effort, fling up a bead out of this funnel-shaped opening, but, even to my limited sense of mechanics, the chances seemed very unfavorable towards it doing much more than roll over the spacious roof into the huge gutters surrounding it.

Yet, if it chose to bound, it might clear the coping and fall, as one had fallen, on the devoted head of a person walking on the lawn below. All this I saw at a glance, and then, sick and dizzy, I crept back, and, with but little apology for my abruptness, took leave of Mrs. Vandyke and left the house.

The resolution I took in doing this was worthy of an older head and a more disciplined heart. By means that were fair, or by means that were foul, I meant to win my way into that boarded-up attic and see for myself if the words hidden away in my vinaigrette were true. To do this openly would cause a scandal I was yet too much under my husband's influence to risk; while to do it secretly meant the obtaining of keys which I had every reason to believe he kept hidden about his person. How was I to obtain them? I saw no way, but that did not deter me from starting at once down town in the hope of being struck by some brilliant idea while waiting for him in his office.

Was it instinct that suggested this, or was the hand of Providence in all that I did at this time? I had no sooner seated myself in the little room, where I had been accustomed to wait for him, than I saw what sent the blood tingling to my finger-tips in sudden hope. It was my husband's vest hanging in one corner, the vest he had worn down town that morning. The day was warm and he had taken it off. *If the key should be in it!*

I had never done a mean or underhanded thing before in my life, but I sprang at that vest without the least hesitation, and fingering it with the lightest of touches, found in the smallest of inside pockets a key, which instinct immediately told me was that of the door I had once endeavored to pass. Oh, the rush of feeling overwhelming me as I held it in my hand! Would he miss it if I carried it off? Would I be able to return to the house, see what I wanted to see, and get back in time to restore it before he wanted his vest? It was early yet, and he was very busy; I might succeed, and if I failed, and he detected his loss, why I alone would be the sufferer; and was I not a sufferer now? Dropping the key into my pocket, I went back into the outer room, and leaving word that I had remembered a little shopping which would take me again up town, I left the building and returned to —— Street. My emotions were indescribable, but I preserved as sedate an appearance as possible, and was able to account for my return in a natural enough way to Ambrose when he opened the door for me. To brave his possible curiosity by going up-stairs, required a still greater effort; but the thought that my intentions were pure and my daring legitimate, sustained me in the ordeal, and I ran, singing, up the first flight, glad that Ambrose had no better ear for music than to be pleased with what he probably considered an evidence of happiness on the part of his young mistress.

I was out of breath with suspense, as well as with my rapid movements, when I reached the shut-in staircase and carefully unlocked its narrow door. But by the time I had reached the fourth floor, and unlocked, with the same key, the only other door that had a streak of light under it, I had gained a certain degree of tense composure born of the desperate nature of the occasion. The calmness with which I pushed open the door proved this—a calmness which made the movement noiseless, which was the reason, I suppose, why I was enabled to suppress the shriek that rose to my lips as I saw that the room had occupants, and that my worst fears were thus realized.

A woman was sitting, with her back to me, at a table, and before her, with her face turned my way, was a young girl in whom, even at first glance, I detected some likeness to myself. Was this why Mr. Allison's countenance expressed so much agitation when he first saw me? The next moment this latter lifted her head and looked directly at me, but with no change in her mobile features; at which token of blindness I almost fell on my knees, so conclusively did it prove that I was really looking upon Mrs. Ransome and her daughter.

The mother, who had been directing her daughter's hands in some needlework, felt that the latter's attention had been diverted.

"What is it, dear?" she asked, with an indescribable mellowness of voice, whose tone thrilled me with a fresh and passionate pity.

"I thought I heard Mr. Allison come in, but he always knocks; besides, it is not time for him yet." And she sighed.

That sigh went through my heart, rousing new feelings and deeper terrors; but I had no time to indulge in them, for the mother turned at the gasp which left my lips, and rising up, confronted me with an amazement which left her without any ability to speak.

"Who is it, mother?" inquired the blind girl, herself rising and beaming upon me with the sweetest of looks.

"Let me answer," I ventured, softly. "I am Mr. Allison's wife. I have come to see if there is anything I can do to make your stay here more comfortable."

The look that passed over the mother's face warned me to venture no further in the daughter's presence. Whatever that mother had suffered, the daughter had experienced nothing but satisfied love and companionship in these narrow precincts. Her rounded cheeks showed this, and the indescribable atmosphere of peace and gladness which surrounded her. As I saw this, and realized the mother's life and the self-restraint which had enabled her to accept the inevitable without raising a complaint calculated to betray to the daughter that all was not as it should be with them, I felt such a rush of awe sweep over me that some of my fathomless emotion showed in my face; for Mrs. Ransome's own countenance assumed a milder look, and advancing nearer, she pointed out a room where we could speak apart. As I moved towards it she whispered a few words in her daughter's ear, then she rejoined me.

"I did not know Mr. Allison was married," were her first words.

"Madame," said I, "*I* did not know we were the guests of a lady who chooses to live in retirement." And opening my vinaigrette, I took out the bead and the little note which had enwrapped it. "This was my first warning that my husband was not what I had been led to consider him," I murmured. "Mrs. Ransome, I am in need of almost as much pity as yourself. I have been married just six days."

She gave a cry, looked me wildly in the face, and then sank upon her knees, lifting up thanks to heaven. "Twenty-four of these notes," said she; "have I written, and flung upward through that lofty skylight, weighted by the beads he left wound about my darling daughter's neck. This one only has brought me the least response. Does he know? Is he willing that you should come up here?"

"I have come at the risk of my life," I quietly answered. "He does not know that I have surprised his secret. He would kill me if he did. Madame, I want to free you, but I want to do it without endangering him. I am his wife, and three hours ago I loved him."

Her face, which had turned very pale, approached mine with a look I hardly expected to encounter there. "I understand," she said; "I comprehend devotion; I have felt it for my daughter. Else I could not have survived the wrong of this incarceration, and my forcible severance from old associations and friends. I loved *her*, and since the knowledge of her affliction, and the still worse knowledge that she had been made the victim of a man's greed to an extent not often surpassed in this world, would have made her young life wretched without securing the least alleviation to our fate, I have kept both facts from her, and she does not know that closed doors mean bondage any more than she knows that unrelieved darkness means blindness. She is absolutely ignorant that there is such a thing as light."

"Oh, madame!" I murmured, "Oh, madame! Show a poor girl what she can do to restore you to your rights. The door is open and you can descend; but that means—— Oh, madame, I am filled with terror when I think what. He may be in the hall now. He may have missed the key and returned. If only you were out of the house!"

"My dear girl," she quietly replied, "we will be some day. You will see to that, I know. I do not think I could stay here, now that I have seen another face than his. But I do not want to go now, to-day. I want to prepare Theresa for freedom; she has lived so long quietly with me that I dread the shock and excitement of other voices and the pressure of city sounds upon her delicate ears. I must train her for contact with the world. But you won't forget me if I allow you to lock us in again? You will come back and open the doors, and let me go down again through my old halls into the room where my husband died; and if Mr. Allison objects—— My dear girl, you know now that he is an unscrupulous man, that it is my money he begrudged me, and that he has used it and made himself a rich man. But he has one spark of grace in him. He has never forgotten that we needed bread and clothes. He has waited on us himself, and never have we suffered from physical want. Therefore, he may not object now. He may feel that he has enriched himself sufficiently to let us go free, and if I must give my oath to let the past go without explanation, why I am ready, my dear; nothing can undo it now, and I am grown too old to want money except for her."

"I cannot," I murmured, "I cannot find courage to present the subject to him so. I do not know my husband's mind. It is a fathomless abyss to me. Let me think of some other way. Oh, madam! if you were out of the house, and could then come——" Suddenly a thought struck me. "I can do it; I see the way to do it—a way that will place you in a triumphant position, and yet save him from suspicion. He is weary of this care. He wants to be relieved of the dreadful secret which anchors him to this house, and makes a hell of the very spot in which he has fixed his love. Shall we undertake to do this for him? Can you trust me if I promise to take an immediate impression of this key, and have one made for myself, which shall insure my return here?"

"My dear," she said, taking my head between her two trembling hands, "I have never looked upon a sweeter face than my daughter's till I looked upon yours to-day. If you bid me hope, I will hope, and if you bid me trust, I will trust. The remembrance of this kiss will not let you forget." And she embraced me in a warm and tender manner.

"I will write you," I murmured. "Some day look for a billet under the door. It will tell you what to do; now I must go back to my husband."

And, with a sudden access of fear, caused by my dread of meeting his eyes with this hidden knowledge between us, I hastened out and locked the door behind me.

When I reached the office, I was in a fainting

condition, but all my hopes revived again when I saw the vest still hanging where I had left it, and heard my husband's voice singing cheerfully in the adjoining room.

CHAPTER VI.

WHILE OTHERS DANCED.

I CANNOT enter into the feelings of this dreadful time. I do not know if I loved or hated the man I had undertaken to save. I only know I was determined to bring light out of darkness in a way that would compromise nobody, possibly not even myself. But to do this I must dazzle him into giving me a great pleasure. A crowd in the —— Street house was necessary to the quiet escape of Mrs. Ransome and her daughter; so a crowd we must have, and how have a crowd without giving a grand party? I knew that this would be a shocking proposition to him, but I was prepared to meet all objections; and when, with every nerve alert and every charm exerted to its utmost, I sat down at his side that evening to plead my cause, I knew by the sparkle of his eye and the softening of the bitter lines that sometimes hardened his mouth, that the battle was half won before I spoke, and that I should have my party whatever it might cost him in mental stress and worry.

Perhaps he was glad to find me given over to folly at a time when he was waiting for a miracle to release him from the net of crime in which he had involved himself; perhaps he merely thought it would please me, and aid him to thus strengthen our position in the social world before taking our flight to a foreign land; but whatever lay at the bottom of his amenity, he gave me *carte blanche* that night for an entertainment that should embrace all his friends and mine and some of Mrs. Vandyke's. So I saw that doubt removed.

The next thing I did was to procure a *facsimile* of his key from the wax impression I had taken of it in accordance with my promise to Mrs. Ransome. Then I wrote her a letter, in which I gave her the minutest directions as to her own movements on that important evening. After which I gave myself up entirely to the business of the party. Certain things I had insisted on. All the rooms were to be opened, even those on the third floor; and I was to have a band to play in the hall. He did not deny me anything. I think his judgment was asleep, or else he was so taken up with the horrible problem presented by his desire to leave the city and the existence of those obligations which made departure an impossibility, that he failed to place due stress on matters which, at another time, might very well seem to threaten the disclosure of his dangerous secret.

At last the night came.

An entertainment given in this great house had aroused much interest. Most of our invitations had been accepted, and the affair promised to be brilliant. As a bride, I wore white, and when, at the moment of going downstairs, my husband suddenly clasped about my neck a rich necklace of diamonds, I was seized by such a bitter sense of the contrast between appearances and the awful reality underlying these festivities, that I reeled in his arms, and had to employ all the arts which my dangerous position had taught me, to quiet his alarm, and convince him that my emotion sprang entirely from pleasure.

Meantime the band was playing and the carriages were rolling up in front. What he thought as the music filled the house and rose in piercing melody to the very roof, I cannot say. *I* thought how it was a message of release to those weary and abused ones above; and, filled with the sense of support which the presence of so many people in the house gave me, I drew up my girlish figure in glad excitement and prepared myself for the ordeal, visible and invisible, which awaited me.

The next two hours form a blank in my memory. Standing under Mrs. Ransome's picture (I *would* stand there), I received the congratulations of the hundred or more people who were anxious to see Mr. Allison's bride, and of the whole glittering pageant I remember only the whispered words of Mrs. Vandyke as she passed with the rest: "My dear, I take back what I said the other day about the effect of marriage upon you. You are the most brilliant woman here, and Mr. Allison the happiest of men." This was an indication that all was going well. But what of the awful morning-hour that awaited us! Would that show him a happy man?

At last our guests were assembled, and I had an instant to myself. Murmuring a prayer for courage, I slid from the room and ran up-stairs. Here all was bustle also—a bustle I delighted in, for, with so many people moving about, Mrs. Ransome and her daughter could pass out without attracting more than a momentary attention. Securing a bundle I had myself prepared, I glided up the second staircase, and, after a moment's delay, succeeded in unlocking the door and disappearing with my bundle into the fourth story. When I came down, the key I had carried up was left behind me. The way for Mrs. Ransome's escape lay open.

I do not think I had been gone ten minutes from the drawing-room. When I returned there, it was to find the festivities at their height, and my husband just on the point of missing me. The look which he directed towards me pierced me to the heart; not that I was playing him false, for I was risking life, love and the loss of everything I prized, to save him from himself; but that his love for me should be so strong he could forget the two tortured hearts above, in the admiration I had awakened in the shallow people about us. But I smiled, as a woman on the rack might smile if the safety of her loved ones depended on her courage, and, nerving myself for the suspense of such a waiting as few of my inexperience have ever been called upon to endure, I turned to a group of ladies I saw near me and began to talk.

Happily, I did not have to chatter long; happily, Mrs. Ransome was quick in her movements and exact in all she did, and, sooner than I expected, sooner, perhaps, than I was prepared for it, the man who attended the front door came to my side and informed me that a lady wished to see me—a lady who had just arrived from the steamer, and who said she was the mistress of the house, Mrs. Ransome.

Mrs. Ransome! The name spread like wildfire, but before any movement was made, I had bounded, in laughing confusion, to my husband's side, and, grasping him merrily by the arm, cried:

"Your expectations have come true. Mrs. Ransome has returned without warning, and to-night she will partake of the supper you have always had served for her."

The shock was as great, perhaps, as ever man received. I knew what it was likely to be, and held him upright, with the seeming merriment in my eyes which I did not allow to stray from his. He thought I was mad, then he thought he was—then I recalled him to the dangers and exigencies of the moment by saying, with forced *naïveté*: " Shall I go and welcome her to this gathering in her own house, or will you do the honors? She may not know *me*."

He moved, but as a statue might move, shot through and through with an electric spark. I saw that I must act, rather than he, so uttering some girlish sentence about the mice and cat, I glided away into the hall, where Mrs. Ransome stood in the nondescript black cloak and bonnet I had provided her from her own wardrobe. She had slipped a few moments before from the house with her daughter, whom she had placed in a carriage, which I had ordered to wait for them directly in front of the lamp-post, and had now re-entered as the mistress returning unexpectedly after a departure of five years. All had been done as I had planned, and it only remained to carry on the farce and prevent its developing into a tragedy.

Rushing up to her, I told her who I was, and, as we were literally surrounded in a moment, added such apologies for the merry-making in which she found us indulging as my wit suggested and the occasion seemed to demand. Then I allowed her to speak. Instantly she was the mistress of the house. Old-fashioned as her dress was, and changed as her figure must have been, she had that imposing bearing which great misfortune, nobly borne, gives to some natures, and feeling the eyes of many of her old friends upon her, she graciously smiled and said that she was delighted to receive so public a welcome. Then she took me by the hand.

" Do not worry, child," she said, " I have a daughter about your age, which in itself would make me lenient towards one so young and pretty. Where is your husband, dear? He has served me well in my absence, and I should like to shake hands with him before I withdraw with my daughter, to a hotel for the night."

I looked up; he was standing in the open doorway leading into the drawing-room. He had recovered a semblance of composure, but the hand fingering the inner pocket, where he kept his keys, showed in what a tumult of surprise and doubt he had been thrown by this unaccountable appearance of his prisoner in the open hall; and if to other eyes he showed no more than the natural confusion of the moment, to me he had the look of a secretly desperate man, alive to his danger, and only holding himself in check in order to measure it.

At the mention she made of his name, he came mechanically forward, and, taking her proffered hand, bowed over it. "Welcome," he murmured, in strained tones; then, startled by the pressure of her fingers on his, he glanced doubtfully up while she said:

"We will have no talk to-night, my faithful and careful friend, but to-morrow you may come and see me at the Fifth Avenue. You will find that my return will not lessen your manifest happiness." Then, as he began to tremble, she laid her hand on his arm, and I heard her smilingly whisper: "You have too pretty a wife for me not to wish my return to be a benefaction to her." And, with a smile to the crowd and an admonition to those about her not to let the little bride suffer from this interruption, she disappeared through the great front door on the arm of the man who for five years had held her prisoner in her own house. *I* went back into the drawing-room, and the five minutes which elapsed between that moment and that of his return were the most awful of my life. When he came back I had aged ten years, yet all that time I was laughing and talking.

He did not rejoin me immediately; he went up-stairs. I knew why; he had gone to see if the door to the fourth floor had been unlocked or simply broken down. When he came back he gave me one look. Did he suspect me? I could not tell. After that, there was another blank in my memory to the hour when the guests were all gone, the house all silent, and we stood together in a little room, where I had at last discovered him, withdrawn by himself, writing. There was a loaded pistol on the table. The paper he had been writing was his will.

"Humphrey," said I, placing a finger on the pistol, "why is this?"

He gave me a look, a hungry, passionate look, then he grew as white as the paper he had just subscribed with his name.

"I am ruined," he murmured. "I have made unwarrantable use of Mrs. Ransome's money; her return has undone me. Delight, I love you, but I cannot face the future. You will be provided for——"

"Will I?" I put in softly, very softly, for my way was strewn with pitfalls and precipices. "I do not think so, Humphrey. If the money you have put away is not yours, my first care would be to restore it. Then what would I have left? A dowry of odium and despair, and I am scarcely eighteen."

"But—but—you do not understand, Delight.

I have been a villain, a worse villain than you think. The only thing in my life I have not to blush for is my love for you. This is pure, even if it has been selfish. I know it is pure, because I have begun to suffer. If I could tell you——"

"Mrs. Ransome has already told me," said I. "Who do you think unlocked the door of her retreat? I, Humphrey. I wanted to save you from yourself, and *she* understands me. She will never reveal the secret of the years she has passed overhead."

Would he hate me? Would he love me? Would he turn that fatal weapon on me, or level it again towards his own breast? For a moment I could not tell; then the white horror in his face broke up, and, giving me a look I shall never forget till I die, he fell prostrate on his knees and lowered his proud head before me.

I did not touch it, but from that moment the schooling of our two hearts began, and, though I can never look upon my husband with the frank joy I see in other women's faces, I have learned not to look upon him with distrust, and to thank God I did not forsake him when desertion might have meant the destruction of the one small seed of goodness which had developed in his heart with the advent of a love for which nothing in his whole previous life had prepared him.

THE END.